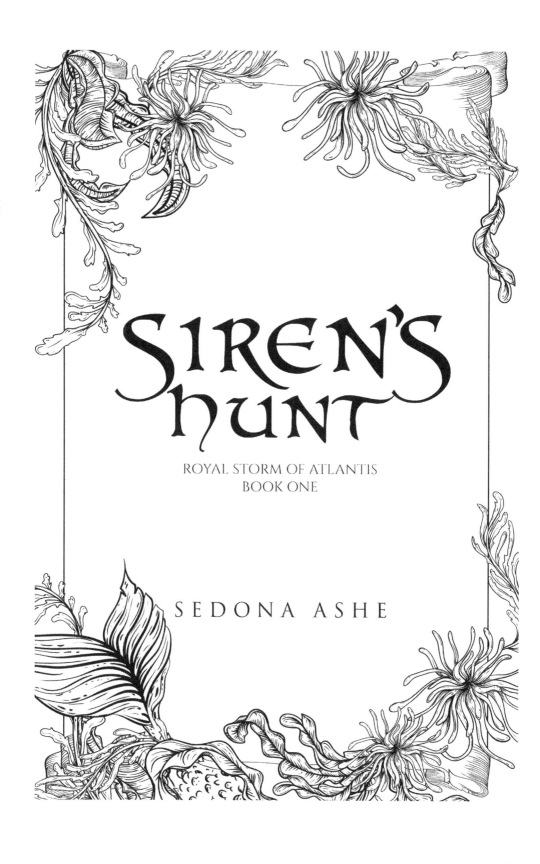

SIREN'S HUNT

ROYAL STORM OF ATLANTIS
BOOK ONE

SEDONA ASHE

CONTENTS

CHAPTER ONE

ZOSIME

I circled beneath a small fishing boat that bobbed on the ocean's surface above me. The moon was mostly hidden behind clouds; the lack of light turned the sea obsidian. Light or no light, I could track my prey with ease thanks to my gifts.

I had been drawn here by the *call*. You would think that taking the longest nap in history would have dulled the strength of the pull. No such luck. It was far worse than I remembered. Of course, that had been centuries ago, so my memory might be foggy.

Echoes of deep male laughter vibrated through the water. For several minutes I clung to the underside of the rocking boat. The man's thoughts slammed into me, nearly causing me to lose my tenuous grip on the boat. I shivered—and it had nothing to do with the dark sea around me. The call drummed in my head, growing louder with each minute I waited. I breathed deeply.

My heartbeat slowed to a steady rhythm in my chest. I knew what had to be done, the same thing that I had done hundreds of times before. I gripped the side of the boat and lifted my upper body from the water. Cold saltwater slid down my face and shoulders, seemingly washing away what little was left of my emotions.

It was time.

I used my arms to brace myself on the edge of the boat.

"Good evening."

At the sound of my soft raspy voice, the loud human male startled. His eyes grew wide, and his breathing shallow as he stared at me. He recovered quickly, swallowing a large gulp of his foul-smelling drink before tossing the can into the sea. It bobbed on the surface alongside several others he had discarded. The humans of this time appear to have little respect for the earth.

He stumbled toward me, a smile curling his lips. "What's a little thing like you doing out here? Did your boyfriend toss you out of his boat for misbehaving?"

I forced an answering smile. Only a few steps further and it would be too late for him. "I need help."

"I'm happy to help, little lady. I think there are some ways you can help me, too." He wiggled his eyebrows suggestively, making sure I didn't miss what he was implying.

One more step.

"Mm." I had never lied, so I found it best to speak to my prey as little as possible. He interpreted my hum as encouragement and took that last fateful step. Leaning down, he brought his face near mine. The putrid smell of his hot breath made me want to gag. Are all human males from this era gross? I would have recoiled, but the call drove me into action.

I threw my arms around his neck, locking them in place. Letting myself fall backward, I yanked him with me. Hard. My momentum knocked him off balance. He uttered a shocked scream and toppled into the sea.

The night was filled with his curses and frantic splashing. On land, his size would have given him an advantage against most women, but he was in my territory now. I took no pleasure in hearing his struggles. I was an efficient hunter. Keeping my arms locked around his neck, I spun around until I was behind him. His cries cut off abruptly when my grip tightened.

He struggled helplessly against my hold. I sank below the surface, allowing the murky depths to engulf me. The man had relaxed in my grip, no longer conscious. His pulse grew fainter with each passing second. The pressure that had steadily built inside me since I first heard tonight's call had turned painful. My stomach clenched in agony. A wave of dizziness blurred my vision. I knew from experience that it would get worse the longer I waited.

My teeth lengthened, allowing me to bite deep into the man's neck. The sour taste of his blood filled my mouth, causing me to gag as I swallowed. His heart gave a final stuttering beat. The pressure inside me released with a pop. It was over.

With a thrust of my powerful fluke, I swam deeper, effort-

3

lessly dragging the large male with me. A shadow passed near me, announcing the arrival of another predator. The shark turned, sleek grey skin gently bumping into me. I had met the magnificent female when I surfaced near the small fishing town several days before. She was a warrior like me.

Having taken what blood I needed, I released the man to the ocean and her subjects.

Tonight's hunt had been successful.

CHAPTER TWO

STORM

"I don't understand why they pulled us from the field to send us to a fishing town in the middle of who-knows-where just to look at the bloated remains of idiots who likely got drunk while fishing and fell overboard." Kye tossed aside the briefing he had been reading.

I looked up from my own copy and met Kye's irritated green gaze. It was ironic that my name was Storm, yet I was the calm one. Kye didn't hide his emotions, and we were never left in the dark about how he felt at any given moment.

Eason spoke without looking up, "Stop being a baby. They want to get a handle on this situation before the media gets ahold of it. There have been eight bodies found over the past month around Apalachee Bay. A predator is hunting there, either on the land or the sea."

Kye gave a snort of derision. "Did you read some of their theories? They suggested it may be an unknown, or long extinct, species of shark! This whole thing sounds like a low budget horror film."

He wasn't wrong. Some of the wild theories were absolutely laughable. However, the alternative was chilling. If it wasn't a sea creature, then a deranged serial killer was stalking the quiet coastline.

I sighed. "They have also called in a marine biologist to analyze the wounds," I responded. "Hopefully there'll be a simple explanation for these deaths."

Kye sighed and slumped back onto the SUV's soft leather seat. "We were so close, Storm. If they hadn't pulled us, we would have had them."

I may not express my emotions as easily as Kye, but they are still there. Anger and disappointment roiled in my stomach. We had been tracking an illegal drilling operation for three years, only to be moved on to this new case.

Orpati was discovered by scientists while exploring uncharted deep sea rock formations five years ago. They took samples of the glowing rock. The world was mesmerized by the beauty of the turquoise stone. When it was found that Orpati could be used as a safe natural energy source, there was a mad rush to mine it as quickly as possible. It was a modern-day gold rush.

Governments fought over mining rights, and for a time it seemed that World War III loomed on the horizon. To prevent a devastating war, an agreement was signed that called a temporary halt to all mining of Orpati. This gave the heads of each country, as well as leading scientists, time to create ethical and fair mining practices.

The small amounts of Orpati that had already been mined become the most valuable resource on earth, subsequently driving the prices up beyond belief. Unfortunately, this led to modern day 'pirating.'

Orpati had been scattered around several thousand miles of the Atlantic Ocean. This made it impossible to fully patrol the area, especially in a world where the rich could buy their own underwater vehicles and robots. Which is exactly what happened.

The rich paid those willing to bend the laws to continue to mine. Since there was no way to distinguish legally mined from illegally mined Orpati, it was easy to sell everything the pirates mined.

The damage these men were doing to the ocean was alarming. Tremors on the ocean floor were being picked up at an increased rate, and a small earthquake had been registered a month before. It was possible that it was simply nature doing her thing, but the scientists were concerned that it was directly related to the crazed mining.

Kye, Eason and I had been working to track the largest of the illegal mining operations. This group had not been careful when mining and had caused some serious damage. We suspected that it was going to trace back to several high-ranking officials inside the government, but we had to obtain concrete proof before pursuing them. Our team had received intel that there would be another mining dive that night, and it would have been a huge break in the case. But that wasn't going to happen now, since we had been sent to investigate a string of mysterious deaths in fishing towns that no one had ever heard of.

On the one hand, I understood why we had been sent. We had spent our lives dedicated to various branches of government and law enforcement. Tracking killers had become a specialty of ours, and our ability to find the most slippery of people had become something we were known for.

However, there was something about the ocean that had always called to each of us, and we spent every minute we were not on a case either in the sea, or studying it. We had dived shipwrecks, caves, archeological sites. Other times we had been included on deep sea exploration trips to the ocean floor, or trips to film and study different ocean species. We had studied the mechanics of ocean drilling, as well as the risks, and had used that knowledge to help implement better options.

Our knowledge of the ocean and advanced military training gave us unique qualifications. This led to our team being brought in on strange and difficult marine cases, both above and below water. I was not surprised our expertise was requested for this string of deaths, but another part of me wondered if the sudden change in assignment had something to do with how close we were getting to the miners. Was it possible that our theories were correct, and that someone had tipped off the higher-ups?

The sound of the car door opening broke me from my thoughts. We had arrived and Kye, who hated being confined, had jumped out before the vehicle had even come to a complete stop. Eason shook his head at Kye's antics, but he wasted no time getting out of the vehicle as well. Our team was always more comfortable in open spaces, preferably surrounded by the ocean.

I stretched my aching muscles and glanced around. The smell of saltwater and driftwood filled my lungs. The small town had an aged look, but it had never been a bustling metropolis. This was the type of place you either retired to, or you were born and raised in.

It seemed we were in the town's center. There was a quaint town hall building that had the sturdy elegance of buildings that had stood for a long time. A gas station with a small deli inside was bustling. That must be the local hangout for lunch. Large trees were scattered around the area draped in moss, they reminded me of creatures from a fantasy movie, as if they would begin to move and talk at any moment.

An officer approached us and quickly introduced himself, "I'm glad you guys have arrived," he said, after offering us all a firm handshake. "The fish guy got here a few minutes ago, so we can explain everything at the same time. Follow me."

The officer turned and moved toward the small building marked by the county medical examiner sign. He didn't bother checking to see if we were following. I got the distinct impression he was eager to get us briefed and hand this case off to us. It was always nice when local law enforcement was friendly, but I didn't think he wanted anything to do with whatever was going on.

The interior was cool and dry, a stark contrast to the stifling humidity and heat of the Florida coastline. My nose burned with the overwhelming chemical scent permeating the air. We stepped into a large open room with several gurneys spread around, each containing a victim. Glancing around the room, I was thankful for the chemicals that had taken my sense of smell.

"Dr. Fynn, the other investigators have arrived," the officer said in the direction of a tall man in a lab coat. "If you want to join us in the meeting room, we'll go over the full briefing." The officer barely glanced the doctor's way before moving into the next room.

Kye snickered behind me. I rolled my eyes, already knowing exactly what he was thinking. "Don't say it, Kye."

"But—"

"No." My tone was firm, but Kye didn't care.

"*Fynn*, like *fin*." He had whispered it, but in the bare room the sound carried.

"Yes, Fynn, like a fish's fin," the doctor chimed in. "I am a marine biologist, with a focus on marine mammals. The perfect name for the job, or so I am constantly being told." The man gave a friendly smile as he strode toward us, not offended in the least by Kye's pun.

"Yes, we are well aware of who you are, Doctor," Kye said. "It's a pleasure to work this case with you."

"Please call me Fynn. If you knew me, you'd know I don't enjoy formality." He laughed and held out his hand.

We shook hands and exchanged names before making our way to the main meeting room where the officer waited with the other county officials. The faces around the room looked exhausted. From my research, outside of natural disasters, the area had not seen this many deaths in a row in its history. These officers were great at their jobs, but this was outside their comfort zone. Who could blame them?

I listened as the officers took turns going over the information they had gathered. My sources had provided all the same details, so I used the time to study the faces around me. If there was a serial killer hunting the area, he or she could very well be in this room.

The cause of death varied among the victims, but it included heart attack, drownings, and apparent shark attacks. They'd all happened within a period of a month, and all the bodies were discovered in the water, nibbled on by various sea inhabitants. In a large city, eight deaths wouldn't have been noticed, but in a community of this size it was alarming.

After the briefing, we followed Dr. Fynn back into the medical examiner's part of the building.

"Now the fun part," Kye groaned. We had all spent time observing autopsies, but it wasn't something I ever looked forward to.

"I only had a few moments to inspect the wounds before the briefing," Fynn said as he slid on a pair of latex gloves. "The first thing I need to do is compare the bite marks. We need to see if it's one species, and possibly one individual of that species, who is conducting most of the attacks. If an aggressive predator is in the area, maybe it's going after anyone that hits the water."

"Do you have a theory on the different causes of deaths?" Eason asked.

"I think it's possible that a shark attack may have been

behind each. The victim could end up in the water, then they see the shark circling and suffer a heart attack from fear. It's also possible that the victims could have drowned during an attack, dying from inhaling water."

"Are you sure it's a shark?" Kye had moved to stand near Fynn and was inspecting a man's leg with a particularly vicious bite. I was surprised the limb was still attached at all.

"Yes, and no," the Doctor replied. "There is definitely a shark involved, but there are a number of other more curious wounds on these bodies. A few of the bites do not match the bite marks of sharks known to inhabit the coastal waters in this area. I'm going to need to take some photos and compare them to other species. Perhaps one has moved into this area."

"What about an alligator?" Kye asked.

Fynn glanced up. "Unlikely, but I guess it's possible."

"Please tell me you don't believe an extinct creature has suddenly emerged like something from a movie." Kye couldn't mask the derision in his tone.

Chuckling, Fynn turned back to the bodies. "I've heard the theories being spread around locally. No, I don't believe that. Although, until we have matched the wounds, nothing is certain. Wouldn't it be amazing to have the chance to study a living member of a long extinct or even completely undiscovered species?"

I had to admit that would be amazing, but we were here to track facts, not conduct a hunt for a cryptid.

It was time to get to work. I turned to the doctor. "Show us how to help."

CHAPTER THREE

ZOSIME

I sped through the ocean, each thrust of my fluke propelling me forward through the murky water. The moon sparkled on the surface like glittering diamonds. It would have been a perfect night to explore the waters I now found myself in, but instead the call had come again. If I wanted peace, I needed to deal with this quickly.

I slowed as the ocean became shallower. Boats of all sizes floated on the surface above me. Debris littered the sand beneath me, with small fish and crustaceans darting among the trash. Carefully, I wove through broken wood crates and submerged netting.

I gagged as I drew in a breath of the filthy water and wished like crazy that I was back in the clear depths far from shore.

Just get it done, and you can go rest.

I tried to give myself a pep talk, but my anxiety continued to climb. Voices from the humans near the docks began to bombard my mind. I could handle one or two voices, but so many voices at once was unbearable.

When I had awakened, I had found myself being pulled by a current from cool waters to these warmer ones. During that journey, a large metal vessel had floated above me. I was still struggling to comprehend the human speech of this time, but I had understood enough to know that they were soldiers. They thought about missions, leaders, training, and battle. All things that I understood well.

The problem was the number of humans that resided on the vessel. There had to have been more than two hundred men, and I could hear every single thought that went through their minds. To escape the mind-shattering pressure, I descended deeper into the icy abyss beneath me, much further than I had ventured before.

Thankfully, my body had adjusted to the drastic change in temperature. My body still shivered, but I hadn't frozen. Another surprise had come when my body had lit up like a lantern as the sea around me turned midnight blue and then obsidian. My scales had pulsed with a soft phosphorescent green light. I had avoided the depths. Just the thought of that absolute darkness and the odd creatures that dwelled there made my insides churn in fear, and the skin on my arms and neck prickle.

While it wasn't an experience I was eager to repeat in the near future, I couldn't deny the peace that had come over me as the voices had faded and my mind quietened. My vision blurred as white-hot pain sliced through my skull and I slammed hard into a wooden beam supporting a dock. The water vibrated with groans from the old wood and my pain.

Letting out a string of curses in a language I imagined was long dead, I began to move forward again, far more cautiously this time. Several male voices cheered and shouted like they were watching fierce gladiators, while their private thoughts were a drunken jumble. Another male shouted orders at the men working on his boat; they obeyed, but their thoughts were filled with nasty comebacks they weren't brave enough to voice aloud. The pressure in my skull built with each passing moment as thoughts of love, heartbreak, sorrow, joy, hope, and anger overwhelmed me.

Desperation bubbled up inside me. I needed to hurry, answer the call, and get the Tartarus away from the humans and their incessant thinking. The number of changes to my body and the world around me were overwhelming. For the past few weeks I had shoved down my panic. I focused on surviving; emotions would have to wait. Hearing the call had been both relieving and terrifying. It was the one single thing that was familiar to me in this new world, but to answer, I had to venture closer to the humans and away from the relative safety of the ocean.

I was near the source of tonight's call. She sat on the peer, her bare feet swayed, kicking up glittering sprays of saltwater. Her thoughts pushed forward from the rest of the din in my brain. Sadness. Rage. The small female hadn't always been this way; something had changed in her life, and it left her open.

Surfacing slowly, I allowed her to see my face. With some of the others this had shocked them, and they had toppled into the water. This girl was not easily scared.

"Haven't you heard?" she said softly. "There's some freaky fish in the water attacking people. The people on the news are telling everyone to stay away from the ocean." She studied the scales on my face, her eyes showing only curiosity.

"Why then do you have your feet in the sea?" My voice was throaty. A lack of speaking and the constant salt of the sea had taken a toll on my vocal cords.

I watched as she threw back her head and laughed, the sound melodious as it filled the humid air around us.

"Maybe I want to meet this predator." Her gaze was steady as it met my eyes. She brought a small metal container to her curled lips and took a long sip.

I sniffed, prepared to feel the burn of the foul-smelling beverage. To my surprise, it didn't come. Squinting at the scribbles on the container I tried to decipher the language. Thanks to my unique heritage and the gifts that came with it, and the thoughts of the humans that forced themselves into my mind, I was catching up quickly with the modern world and the language spoken in this area. I recognized the individual letters on the can but couldn't yet read them as words.

"It's called soda." She answered my unspoken question. "Here, try one. It's a sugar drink with caffeine."

I caught the can she tossed to me, some of the bubbly liquid sloshing out. My head pounded mercilessly from the call, but my curiosity got the best me. Lifting the can, I took a careful sniff before cautiously taking a sip. It was unlike anything I had tasted before. The sweet beverage tickled my tongue and throat as I swallowed.

"Pretty good, right? I'm Yashy, by the way."

"Yes. Strange, but not unpleasant. I'm Zosime."

"So, you're the one killing off the people around the bay?"

Her tone was indifferent, as if she didn't really care about the answer. How was I supposed to respond? I had never told a lie; I would not start with this female. I simply nodded, sipping more of the syrupy drink.

"Huh. Why? Just for fun? Or is there a deeper reason?" She leaned toward me. I wished she would lean away; the call drummed louder with each passing moment.

"I swore an oath to answer the call," I replied firmly. "It pulls me where I am needed, to where the Lure has taken hold and eroded. Please, you could turn back."

Even as I spoke the last words, I knew it was too late. Her thoughts of knives, pain, and revenge ran in circles in my mind. She had been hurt beyond what a human should ever have to bear. The Lure had eroded away every bit of human decency from the men who had tormented her and left her broken. In turn, she had allowed the Lure to seep into her soul and numb her pain. She had served up her revenge with an ice-cold heartlessness that was both terrifying and inspiring.

"I can't though," Yashy replied. "I made my decision knowing what that meant for me. Those men paid, and they will never touch another human again. The desire for blood-lust hasn't died along with them though, but I don't want to hurt someone. I've gone past the point of return, but I don't regret my decision for a single second."

Her words held a touch of sadness, but her lips and eyes twinkled at her remembered revenge.

"Alright, so what's next?" she said with a sigh, turning to face me. "Do you morph into something terrifying? Do I jump in the water? Do you sing? Ugh, please don't tell me you sing country music." She yanked free the two bloody knives she had stabbed into the wooden dock and tossed them into the ocean.

I had never taken a willing victim, not in all my time on earth, and my hesitation must have been written on my face.

"Zosime, you know your job, and I know that I cannot fight the evil inside of me forever." Yashy looked at me with pleading eyes. "Please, I'm tired."

"I will make it quick. If I knew of a cure—"

"We both know this isn't your everyday kind of bad vibe. I'm sure you know more about it than me, but I can feel it consuming me like a plague. This is a curse, and it isn't human."

She had no idea how correct she was. It wasn't human, it was created with the magik of an Ancient. I thought of how many from the human population were now contaminated, and it distressed me. Was I the only one left of the Promised? Had anyone been working on a cure to combat the Lure?

I was yanked from the thoughts as Yashy plunged into the water next to me. I caught her arm and held her head above water.

"Let's go for a swim, mermaid!" She continued to laugh as

my fangs descended. We slowly sank beneath the sea, the cool water a contrast to the fiery rage that burned inside me.

In another life, I'd have liked having this tiny warrior female as my friend. Yet one more thing this cruel world had stolen from me.

Also, what is a mermaid?

CHAPTER FOUR
STORM

I slid my sunglasses on as we stood around the body of the latest victim. The morning light was painfully bright as the sun rose and glinted across the water. An early morning jogger had found the body of the young female.

"It just doesn't make sense." Fynn kneeled in the sand beside the body. "I spent most of the night studying the different wounds on each body. This female only has one wound, the single bite to her neck. There are no other obvious signs of trauma to the body."

"Does the bite match any of the bites on the other victims?" Eason stepped forward, looking over Fynn's shoulder.

"Yes," Fynn replied. "But it's the one bite that doesn't match any known species, which means we still don't know who, or what, killed them." Fynn rocked back on his heels, a frown on his face.

"I wonder what made this kill different," Eason mused. "The others were found in the water and had been nibbled on by local sea life. She is the first to be found dry on the shore. If it weren't for the obvious bite mark, I wouldn't have guessed she was linked to the other victims." Eason leaned in for a closer look at that telltale bite, before turning to Kye. "Have we gotten the full backgrounds on each victim?"

"They sent them to us last night, but the files were bare," Kye replied. "It seems the locals were hesitant to include the full details for each person. I'm guessing there are some small-town politics at play. I put in a call to my guy back at the base, and he'll be sending backgrounds within the next few hours. By the time he finishes, we'll know if they so much as jaywalked."

I nodded at Kye, appreciating the fact he had already taken care of this. My team worked smoothly and efficiently; everyone pulled their weight.

"What can you tell us about the bite, Fynn?" I asked the doctor.

He walked toward me, slipping on his own pair of sunglasses. "The more I study it, the more confused I become. Without doubt, it's the bite of a predator. It's strange, closer to a human's bite mark than the mark of any marine species I've studied. Both the canine teeth and the lateral incisors are longer than the other teeth. It also appears that there's a smaller row of teeth behind the larger teeth."

"Are you sure it isn't a shark? They have multiple rows of teeth." Kye asked the obvious.

"I can't be positive until I am able to exam the predator myself, but the second row is different than the known shark species. Perhaps it's a deformed shark, but that wouldn't explain the clean bite this victim has on her neck. There would be torn flesh, but this is a clean impression. Hopefully the medical examiner can figure out the cause of death."

My gaze was drawn to the expansive ocean. Waves lapped at the shore, scattering seaweed and shells along the beach.

Suddenly, I was overcome by a strange and powerful urge. *Closer.*

The need to move toward the ocean was sudden and demanding. I always felt the call of the ocean when I was near it. I longed to slip on my fins and find peace under the surface. But this was a pull so strong that I moved automatically toward the water. My feet stumbled as I was pulled between the urge to obey and the desire to fight the irrational demand. I was working, this was not the time to enjoy a quick dip.

Eason's hand clamped down on my shoulder. "Are you okay, man?"

I staggered to a halt. "Uh, yeah. I'm fine. It's probably just jetlag."

He looked at me with a serious expression. "You feel the urge to swim too, don't you?" His voice was barely above a whisper.

"Yes," I said, frozen in place. "It's so strong that I am afraid to move at all." I couldn't hide the tension in my voice. This wasn't normal.

A splashing sound to my left startled me from the trance and I snapped my head in the direction of the noise. Kye must have felt it too because he now stood knee deep in the foamy sea. Eason and I covered the ground between us in a few short strides, stopping just shy of soaking our shoes.

"Kye! Kye!" we called.

His eyes were full of longing when he turned his head toward us. "I thought I saw something, or someone, in the water. Maybe it was just sea grass."

I shook my head in disbelief. What was going on? I couldn't fight the feeling that we had been watched from the moment we stepped onto the beach, but I didn't want to worry the guys by mentioning my own paranoia, so I remained silent.

"Is everything okay over here?" An officer walked toward us, eyeing Kye like he was an idiot.

"It's fine, officer," I said. "Our colleague thought he saw something and wanted to make sure it wasn't a piece of evidence." I turned to Kye in the water, then to Eason. "Let's head back."

As we walked back, we saw that the body was being loaded into the back of the coroner's van. Fynn joined us as we headed toward our rented SUV. It was odd that we had known him for less than twenty-four hours, yet somehow, he seemed to fit into our team like a missing puzzle piece. We had worked with men and women around the world for many years. Their backgrounds had ranged from academia to law enforcement, military to the tough-as-nails working class, and we had managed to do our jobs and work well with them all.

But they were outsiders, never part of our team. Until we arrived here and met Fynn.

This case got weirder with every passing hour. The hair on my neck rose and I could feel eyes on me even as I opened my car door, but not from the bystanders outside the tape. No, I was being watched from the ocean.

The sooner we wrapped this up, the better.

"Do you think we'll actually catch the creature in action?" Kye tossed me a water bottle as he spoke.

"I don't know, but I can't sit idle in the hotel room waiting for another body to show up."

Fynn and Eason leaned against the railed sides of the small boat. We had moved a little way from shore, hoping we might be able to hear any screams in our vicinity. It was a long shot, but we didn't have a lot of options at that moment.

Fynn's phone vibrated, and he checked the notification. "It looks like we got some preliminary reports back on the latest victim. The body showed signs of long-term trauma, but the wounds were old or nearly healed." He paused and seemed to zoom in on something on his screen. "Huh. That's odd. There are traces of a toxin in her bloodstream."

"What type of toxin?" Eason asked. "She ingested something?" He leaned toward Fynn's phone. He had spent years studying toxins and had a bit of an obsession with them. To my surprise, Fynn angled his phone toward Eason, allowing him to read the report at the same time.

"It's a neurotoxin called tetrodotoxin, or TTX," Fynn explained. "The blue-ringed octopus is the only thing with a comparable bite, but the marks don't match. This venom is no joke—it's one of the deadliest venoms found in the ocean. If bitten, death would be quick. A victim wouldn't even realize they needed medical help until it was too late. Not that medical help would save them anyway." He sounded more fascinated than horrified.

"Did they find traces of the toxins in any of the other victims?" Kye asked the question before I could voice it.

"That's the odd thing, it's only in the latest victim," Fynn replied. "If it weren't for the distinct and unique bite imprint, I wouldn't have believed this victim was killed by the same predator."

Eason leaned back against the rail, crossing his arms and wrinkling his brow. "It almost seems like this girl was killed with mercy. Which is impossible since this is an animal, right?"

"Right..." Fynn elongated the word, his voice trailing off. He pinched his brow and sighed.

"Any idea what we're looking for?" I asked, but I didn't expect an answer.

Kye's laughter broke the quiet of the night. "A mermaid! Not the cute cartoon type of mermaids, but the type that lure sailors to their death."

Eason smacked Kye on the back of his head, cutting Kye's laughter off abruptly.

"Ow, man. What was that for?"

"I was trying to knock some sense into you, fool."

A chill slammed into the boat, and the hair on my neck rose. The night had been hot and humid, without so much as a breeze. I looked to the other guys, but they looked just as confused. Eason and Kye had dropped their easy-going banter and had taken up defensive stances.

I waited for another gust, but it never came. Around us, the night was calm. Unnaturally calm. The water's surface was still, a perfect glass mirror. Not a single wave broke the illusion.

"There's something fishy going on," Kye whispered.

Fynn and I groaned in amused exasperation. Eason gave Kye a playful shove. Unfortunately, it was a bit harder than he had intended. Kye stumbled, losing his footing. Eason grabbed for Kye's shirt but missed, clutching at thin air instead. Kye tumbled off the back of the boat, his head made a sickening crack against the small platform at the boat's stern. He hit the water with a crash and sunk below the surface.

Another splash sounded from nearby. My stomach dropped like lead. Whatever made that splash was much larger than a normal fish.

A predator was in the water.

CHAPTER FIVE

ZOSIME

The four men in the fishing vessel talked and joked, the music of their laughter reaching me even beneath the surface of the water. I had been drawn here, but it had nothing to do with the call.

That morning I had hidden in the reeds, watching to ensure the female had been found. She was brave and deserved to be treated with respect. Emotion stirred in my chest when I thought of her. Even before the battle that sent Atlantis into the sea and me into suspended animation, my emotions were dulled.

I had sworn to fight the Lure that was spreading across earth. To do my job properly, I couldn't be distracted by emotions. The call led me to my targets, to those with souls already damaged by the Lure. Some were evil and had done despicable things, making it easy to complete my mission. Others were like the female, Yashy—good humans that the Lure preyed on. The mission had to be completed regardless. There was no coming back from the Lure, but emotions made it harder to kill those whose souls weren't completely eroded away.

The Ancients took pity on the Promised, and buried our emotions, giving us the ability to destroy the Lure without hesitation. Once the Lure was defeated, we were to have our full emotions restored. It clearly wasn't defeated, so why were my emotions trying to surface?

The female had been found quickly that morning. I was forced to remain still in the water to avoid detection. They wouldn't have been able to catch me in the water, but a hunt would have started. I wasn't ready for that, not yet. As more officers and bystanders arrived on the beach, my head pounded with the chaotic thoughts.

Just when I thought my skull might crack from the pressure, a man had walked on the beach. He wasn't as tall as the Atlantean guards, but he carried himself in a way that made him seem taller than the rest of the men on the shore. Unlike the other men, his hair brushed against his shoulders. It was the pale color of the sand, a contrast to his tanned skin. This man spent long hours outside, not hidden away from the sun.

The closer he came to the water's edge, the more the pressure in my mind eased. I was still in pain, but the sharp edge had softened. The man moved around the body, paying special attention to my bite mark on her neck. I wondered what he had thought about it. Would he recognize the bite? Were there others out there like me?

The arrival of three more men caused a shift among everyone on the beach. Their presence commanded attention without them speaking a word. These men could have stood proudly among the Atlantean warriors. People avoided eye contact, and unconsciously moved out of their way. Everyone reacted, except for the man studying the bite mark. His body remained relaxed, even when the others moved close enough to peer over his shoulder.

The pain in my mind eased a little more. The voices were still there, but quieter. My heart did a strange flutter in my chest, and I had to search my memory to recall the sensation. I had felt this once before, before I became a Promised and swore my life to destroying the Lure. Centuries had passed, but I would never forget him or that single day we had spent in a haze of passion. Now these four men had my heart stirring and my body desiring things that made my cheeks flush.

I remained motionless, but somehow the men sensed my presence. The man with the easy smile and eyes the same color as sea grass had strode into the water in a trance. His eyes were searching, although he had no idea what he was looking for. I knew humans were drawn to me, but only after seeing me. This new form gave me an allure I had yet to figure out. Why were these men feeling it without even seeing me?

A sense of longing washed through me, stealing my breath and forcing salty tears from my eyes. I couldn't stay here any longer. I carefully sank to the shallow seabed, hoping that would cover my retreat. It took several long minutes to ease myself into deeper water since I didn't want to risk an accidental splash of my large fluke.

I spent the remaining hours of daylight resting in a small sea cave I had found. There wasn't a lot of room to move around, but I like the security it provided me. I preferred sunlight (the Atlanteans were a people who thrived in the sun) but it also increased the risk that I would be spotted.

There was only so long I could remain hidden. I had work to do and an oath to keep. At some point, I needed to make contact with the humans of this time and figure out what had happened during the years I was asleep. The problem was figuring out who to approach. I didn't relish the idea of becoming someone's dinner, trophy, or pet, and I wasn't sure how the humans would react to me. The female had been kind, but the others had been cruel, and their thoughts corrupt. I had yet to speak with a human that the Lure hadn't touched. Maybe I needed to approach the men from the beach. Perhaps that was the reason for my pull toward them.

That is how I ended up watching their boat from a small rock outcropping. I was hidden, but able to observe them. Their thoughts pushed at my mind, and instead of trying to stifle them, I opened my mind, allowing their voices to fill my mind. I needed to know more about these men. The Lure hadn't touched them, but that didn't mean they were good. There was evil in the world that had nothing to do with the magik of the Lure. It was possible to be one without the other.

The men's laughter echoed across the water, sending warm tingles through my body. The largest of the men, I heard them call him Eason, reached out a hand with impressive speed and slapped the emerald-eyed man who was called Kye. Unexpected anger surged through me with a force so strong it forced a startled exhalation from me. What was even more shocking was my breath transforming into a gust of wind that rushed across the water and slammed into the small vessel. I clung to the rock, limp and confused.

The men had just been joking. They were like brothers, relaxed and comfortable with one another. Their playful exchange shouldn't have caused me to feel anger; I wasn't supposed to be able to feel any emotions that strong.

I didn't like to see anyone touch what was mine.

The realization made even less sense. Yes, I was curious about them, that's why I was stalking them. But they weren't mine, they were strangers. My mother had told me stories of instant bonding, but it was a myth, not something I had ever seen happen among my people. I couldn't be feeling a bond with strangers, could I? They were humans, and I was... I didn't even know what I was.

My body had continued to adapt and change since my wake-up call. Tonight, I had manipulated the air around me. What if I did it again and hurt an innocent? Or gave away my location? Atlanteans possessed gifts, but nothing that would explain the continued changes I was experiencing.

I focused back on the men. Their expressions were serious, and their thoughts told me they worried for the safety of the humans. It seemed they didn't know what had caused the deaths, but they were determined to figure it out. They had been sent here specifically to hunt down the killer, whether it was a human or an animal. The fact that I was neither might have been funny if I hadn't been just as clueless as to what I'd become.

"There's something fishy going on," the man named Kye had whispered.

I had laughed before quickly clamping a hand over my mouth. I hadn't laughed since I awoke, and even in my previous life I remembered laughing only on rare occasions. I didn't get time to dwell on this latest development. A crack, followed by a heavy splash, yanked my focus to the disturbed water at the back of the boat. Ducking my head beneath the water I searched for the human, expecting to see him kicking back to the surface with a smile on his face.

Instead, I saw Kye's limp body sinking like stone toward the seabed, twenty feet below the vessel. The coppery taste of his blood sent my body and mind into a tailspin. Sharks weren't the only creature of the deep who could taste blood in the water. I wanted to save him from drowning, but I also wanted to sink my fangs into his neck and taste him. My new nature required blood to survive, but I hadn't craved blood in the way that I wanted Kye's.

All thoughts of staying hidden fled from my mind. I wanted him safe, and I wanted to taste him. I shot like a torpedo through the water, not bothering to hide the sounds of my fluke as I used it to propel myself faster than I had ever moved before.

Mine. Mine. Mine.

Sand and silt puffed around him like a cloud when he landed with a soft thump on the seafloor. He remained motionless, a thin line of crimson blood drifting up from his head. His team shouted out orders, I could hear them scrambling for the back of the boat. They were going to jump in as well.

I had nearly reached him when a silver glimmer caught my attention. The panic inside me tripled and I forgot to breathe. I wasn't the only predator in these waters tonight, and the large female shark that I had grown fond of had smelled the blood as well. She must have been nearby to have arrived this fast.

I was faster than her, but I wasn't sure if I could outrun her while carrying a body. The beautiful female didn't deserve to be attacked for simply existing in her own habitat and eating what was available in the ocean. I wasn't sure I could take her down without a weapon, even if I had been willing to.

If the men jumped in, she was going to have more than one target and I couldn't keep them all safe. I could try to toss him up on the boat and then get out of there. That was the best choice, the logical choice. But I couldn't do it. He was mine and he was hurt. I needed to be with him, and I didn't think they would trust me. With the way my gums ached, I wasn't sure I trusted me completely either.

I wrapped my arms around Kye's lifeless body and thrust my fluke hard to send us hurtling toward the surface. Our heads broke the water, and I rushed to expel the water from my lungs. I could breathe above or below the water, but I couldn't communicate with humans with water-logged lungs. Despite this, I still struggled to speak.

"His...his heart beats. I will not harm him. There is a large shark heading for the boat. Do not enter the water tonight."

I didn't give them time to react. Leaving them frozen in stunned disbelief, I sank beneath the waves again. I had to get Kye out of the water so I could get him breathing. I knew just the place, but first I had to outrun a hungry shark who had just realized that I had stolen her meal.

I swam like my life depended on it, and maybe it did. My heart told me that I might not make it if the stranger in my arms died. My teeth had lengthened and need began to pound out a beat that matched the frantic pounding of my heart. He was being hunted by two predators tonight. I might not be able to save him from both.

I pulled his body tighter against mine, trying to reduce the drag as much as possible. My powerful fluke displaced enormous amounts of water, surging me forward. My body undulated, but my companion's limp body made my movements jerky. Glancing over my shoulder, I saw that the sleek queen of the bay had turned from the boat and was streaking toward me. Her entire body was built for speed and efficiency in the water, so it wasn't a surprise that she was closing the gap between us horrifyingly fast.

Gritting my teeth, I dug deep inside me, and something shifted in my chest. Water curled and spun around us, and my burning muscles moved through the water without any strain. We were being sucked along a current. A current that just so happened to be taking me exactly where I wanted. I would have been more concerned over the fact that I now had the ability to manipulate water, but in that moment all I felt was relief.

I bolted into the stone opening next to my cave. My scales shimmered, bathing the dark tunnel in eerie green light. The sharp cave walls angled upwards, and I followed the curve without slowing. We shot up out of the water, slamming hard into damp earth and cool stone. I had moved fast, but Kye had still been underwater for ninety seconds. Wasting no time, I rolled him over and began working to clear water from his lungs.

Water bubbled from his mouth, but he didn't take in a breath. I slammed my fists against his chest and snarled in frustration. Leaning down, I pressed my warm lips against his pale ones. The coolness of his open mouth was a stark contrast to the burning heat of my own. We were both motionless; the moment frozen in time.

A soft gurgle came from his throat, and I jerked back. Nothing happened. Kye remained still. I wanted to see his playful smile and bright green eyes. I reached out and brushed a finger along his stubbled jawline. Water trickled from the corner of his mouth, but instead of submitting to gravity and slipping to the ground, it moved toward my finger that rested against his jaw.

In disbelief, I slid my finger up his cheek. The water trailed after my finger like an obedient pup. Lifting my finger away, I held it several inches above his face. Water followed my finger like a snake responding to a charmer. I dropped my hand, absolutely dumbfounded. The thin stream of water fell to the ground.

Clarity smacked me in the face. Moving forward, I pressed my hands against his chest where I guessed his lungs would be. Focusing hard, I thought about what I wanted the water to do and crossed my fins that it would work.

I moved my hands up, trying not to be distracted by the incredible feel of the hard muscular planes of his chest. My body flushed with desire, missing the note that this was not the time.

My hands slid along the column of his neck and along his jawline to his mouth. Water gurgled and bubbled out of his mouth again. Keeping my hands steady, I lifted them away from his mouth and toward me. The water began to rush from his lungs, following my motions. It splashed against me, soaking the ground around me.

Kye choked, automatically rolling to his side. Powerful coughs wracked his body as he worked to clear the remaining water from his lungs. I scooted toward him, patting his back and supporting him as he propped himself up. It took several minutes before his breathing grew less raged and more natural.

He lifted his shirt hem, rubbing at his face. The damp material did nothing to dry his face, and when I caught a peek of his abs, the shirt wasn't the only thing that was wet. I wanted to smack myself. Sure, it had been centuries—fine, millennia—since I had felt my body intertwined with a man. But that was no reason to be this easily aroused.

I bit my lip and tasted blood. The sharp tips of my fangs were still strange to me, and I forgot about them far too often. In this moment I was struggling to hang onto the human traits

I had learned. It was futile attempt because I wasn't fully human. I was beginning to question if I was human at all.

With a pained groan, Kye turned toward me. He took in my appearance for the first time. His eyes grew round, and his pupils dilated until the green of his irises disappeared. Chaotic thoughts tumbled through his mind while he tried to make sense of his current situation—and me. I waited, not wanting to admit how much I dreaded hearing his reaction out loud. But nothing on this earth could have prepared me for his reaction.

The tension in his face eased, and his heart slowed from erratic to only slightly faster than normal. He lifted his arm and rubbed the back of his neck in an adorable, but practiced, gesture that was designed to show off his toned abs. His biceps flexed as he moved, affecting me more than it should. I was a warrior that had trained among gladiators without my body reacting. Yet this human man with the kind smile, boyish charm, and gentle thoughts, was stirring the desire to hunt inside me. The desire to hunt and devour him. My mouth watered.

Through the eyes of a predator, I watched him catch his lower lip between his teeth for moment, biting gently before letting go. I stopped breathing, unable to look away. His chest rumbled as he spoke, his voice a deeper pitch than I had heard him use before. Was the human male attempting to lure me with his voice, just as I had done with several of my recent victims?

"Hey baby, are you a mermaid or am I the one who made you all wet?"

CHAPTER SIX

KYE

How hard had I hit my head? I remembered making a joke about mermaids, Eason giving me a playful shove, and then whacking my head as I tumbled off the boat. But I don't remember going into the water. Although, from the water I had coughed up and my soaked clothing, it was obvious that I had not only fallen into the water, but I had nearly died.

Where were the guys? Shouldn't they be here trying to save me? I turned to look for them, and locked eyes with a— mermaid? I was dreaming. Maybe I was still unconscious. That explained the strange cavern and my missing friends. The last thing I had said before losing my footing was a joke about mermaids, and my mind had conjured one.

Long dark hair fell down her back, hiding much of her

face and body. Glowing eyes watched me from behind the curtain of hair. When I say glowing, I mean they literally glowed. The effect reminded me of the golden light reflecting in a cat's eyes in the dark, except her eyes glinted turquoise, the color of Caribbean waters.

I followed the damp strands of her hair down her body. Her skin was pale, shimmering scales, the same color as her eyes, and they pulsed in a faint rhythm. It took me a minute to realize why the sight was familiar, why I was convinced that I had seen a similar light show. Then I remembered my work with a research team at a large aquarium. I had spent a summer studying bioluminescence in jellyfish. Their mesmerizing display had caused the entire team to lose track of time on more than one occasion. This affect, now on the mermaid, only added to her allure.

My eyes drifted lower and came to a halt. Books and movies normally portrayed mermaids as having either shells or seaweed styled into a bra, or being completely topless. Turns out they all had it wrong. The reality was more like the armor given to females in video games. You know, the kind that appeared more sexy than practical. A thick piece of 'armor' covered her breastplate and sternum. Smaller individual pieces protected her ribs and connected to the sternum, creating an elegant draping design.

The armor was black and red, but I couldn't figure out what it was made from. I would have guessed leather, but that wouldn't be a logical choice for a sea dweller. I wanted to reach out and explore her body with my hands, not just my eyes. If I was being honest with myself, I didn't just want to explore her body for science. No, I was being drawn to her, ignoring the pull was becoming increasingly difficult with each passing second. It was as impossible as resisting gravity.

Water droplets slid down her body, and my eyes trailed after them. Trepidation and excitement warred inside me. It wasn't every day, or every dream, that you got the chance to study a mermaid. Her skin shifted colors when it came to her hips, the transition from her pale skin to the charcoal of her tail was smooth and gradual. She hadn't just slipped into a tail from the internet to indulge in her own fantasy. No, she was the real deal. The fluke was submerged in the water at the center of the cave, so admiring it would have to wait.

Our eyes locked, and I sucked in a breath as I watched her pupils shift back and forth between rounded and slitted. She wasn't like the mermaids of my daydreams. She was more than I could imagine. Emotion surged inside me, things I thought you could only feel for someone you had known for years. How could you feel so strongly for someone you just met? If I'd had a ring, I would have proposed on the spot. I wasn't going to waste this opportunity, even if it was just a figment of my imagination.

I opened my mouth and the voice that came out was one I didn't recognize. She was affecting every part of me.

"Hey baby, are you a mermaid, or am I the one who made you all wet?"

I wanted to jump back on the boat so I could knock myself out again. Sure, I may be obsessed with cheesy pickup lines, but that one had come out of nowhere. Where had I even heard it?

I watched her reaction and prayed she couldn't speak English. Her aquamarine eyes shimmered with intelligence, and her head tilted as she worked to decipher something. Scales began to flicker, colors flashing like lightning while traveling along her body in a brilliant display. Intuitively, I recognized it as a visual display of her emotions, but couldn't figure out if it was fear, anger, curiosity, or something else.

"You desire me?" The words were spoken in the low sultry tone of a 1950's female blues singer. Her voice hit me like a bolt of electricity, surging through my body and leaving a burning path of desire in its wake.

I huffed out a laugh. "Sweetheart, you have no idea. Yes. Yes, I want you so much it hurts, and that isn't just a figure of speech."

Again, her head tilted as she thought over my words. She worried her bottom lip between her teeth—fangs.

She has fangs.

This wasn't a mermaid, this was a Siren. And if the legends were anything to go by, I was sharing a tiny cavern with the most devious and accomplished predator of the sea. If she decided to attack me, my larger size wasn't going to be enough to save me.

She started to move forward but stopped and glanced down at her tail. I wondered if her hesitation was due to the weight of her tail and fluke. Once that was pulled from the water, the weight would likely be significant. It would slow her down giving me a bit more of a fighting chance should she decide to attack. On the flip side, it would make her more vulnerable, and I doubted that was something she would be okay with.

I hated to think of her feeling uncomfortable, even if I knew she had no reason to fear me. Moving slowly, I scooted toward her. Glinting eyes lifted at my movement, and a predator stared back at me. My heart tripped over its own beat for a split second, but then I remembered this was a dream and you couldn't really die in a dream. At least, I hoped you couldn't.

Inch by excruciatingly slow inch I edged toward her. I stopped when my leg brushed against her thigh. I wondered about the skeletal structure of a mermaid. Did she have two thigh bones? Silencing my inner scientist yet again, I reached out, brushing her check with my knuckles. I couldn't hide the small tremor in my hand as it shook in much the same way it would if I were petting a wild tiger.

She stiffened but remained still. I didn't get bit, so I took that as a good sign. Cupping her face in my palm, I stroked her cheek with my thumb, enjoying the contrast of her slick scales against my roughened skin. Some of the tension left her body and she relaxed into my touch.

"May I kiss you?" I wish I could say my voice came out sexy and confident, but the truth was that the words were little more than a whisper.

Glowing eyes watched me steadily. Her pupils had stopped shifting shapes and now remained slitted like the eyes of a cat. It should have freaked me out more. Maybe I just had a previously unknown kink for the dangerous because something about the unnatural beauty of her predatory features had my body burning with a need like nothing I had experienced before. I wanted her, even if having her was the last thing I would ever do.

"Yes."

My heart soared at that single word. Leaning in, I pressed my lips to the curve of her jawline. Wanting to savor every second of this incredible illusion, I kissed my way to the corner of her mouth, my pace unhurried. Her breathing hitched and she shivered. I smiled, knowing that she was experiencing the same crazy desire that was currently threatening to burn my insides to ash.

I caught her bottom lip between my own, sucking gently. The salty taste of her skin was a reminder that this wasn't your typical kiss. Another taste met my tongue, one that I couldn't place. It was sweet like nectar or honey. My body trembled with desire. I should have been embarrassed to be so affected by simply kissing her, but I didn't care about anything but making her my own at that moment.

Her lips began to move with mine, and our kiss took a turn from sweet to steamy. A soft little hum escaped her mouth, the sound vibrating through me. Dizziness washed over me. The sensation was that of holding your breath for too long, then releasing it and desperately gulping in lungfuls of air. Except in this case, it was her that had me gasping in need. If things stopped at that point, I'm sure I would have passed out.

I needed more. Sliding my hand into her hair, I pulled her lips more firmly against my own. Her hands trailed up my water-soaked shirt. It clung to my skin, and she traced along the lines of my chest through the fabric.

When she sighed out another hum, blood rushed to my groin with a suddenness that caused me to jerk. The movement caught us both off-guard and she nicked my lip with her fang. We both froze. The faint acidic taste of blood was in my mouth, which meant she likely tasted it too. Would she turn full predator now and eat me? Somehow, instead of the thought dousing my desire like cold water, it turned me on even more. Sweat trickled down my forehead and spine, not from fear, but from desire.

"I am sorry. This is not normal for me. I cannot resist any longer." Her soft textured voice trembled.

If she was going to go all predator, I was more than happy to go out this way. Just so long as I got to have her as my last meal.

"Whatever you need, babe. I'm yours." I wasn't the type to make promises and declarations of love during sex, but in that moment, I knew without a doubt that she would have my heart until the day it stopped beating. Whether that was five minutes from now, when she ripped it out and ate it, until I died as an old man, or until I woke up from this way-too-real dream.

She wasted no time, lunging forward, her arms wrapping around my neck. Yanking hard and popping her fin to push herself off the ground a few inches, she twisted me around. I landed with a soft thud on the ground, surprised to find she had moved her hand to the back of my head to ensure it didn't bang against the stone floor of the tiny cavern. A thoughtful gesture that made me think that she might not be planning to eat me. Why would she care if her dinner was braindead?

Her hips and fin settled between my legs, and her hands slid under my shirt. The skin-to-skin contact sent another wave of dizziness through me. How hard had I hit my head? She shimmied, attempting to pull herself up my body. Grabbing her waist, I hauled her up my body until our faces met. The delicious friction of her wiggling body against my erection was a special kind of torture.

She kissed my lips again and then pulled away before I could deepen the kiss. Sucking and licking, she nuzzled her way down my neck. My heavy-lidded eyes jerked open wide when a sting of pain shot through my neck. She had bitten me, and her teeth were still embedded in my skin. As quickly as the pain had come, it disappeared. Instead, lust slammed into me like a tsunami.

This wasn't your typical lust-filled haze. No, this was the type of lust that made you feel like ripping your clothes off and going at it like an animal. Pure, unadulterated, raw need. Imagine being bitten by a venomous animal and feeling the venom move through your body, affecting nerves and muscles, and burning you up on the inside? The only thing that can save you is antivenom, otherwise you'll die. In my case, lust was burning through my body, and I was confident I wouldn't survive if I didn't get to sink inside her and feel her body wrapped around mine.

My mouth was dry, my heartbeat erratic, and my breathing shallow. My erection jerked against the constraints of my pants. Her soft sucking sound just below my ear hit caused my stomach to flip as though we had just gone into zero gravity.

"Please. I need you." If the guys ever found out that I had begged her, I would be ribbed for the rest of my life. I didn't care. But nothing mattered in that moment except her. The only problem was that I wasn't sure how exactly a mermaid, or whatever this sexy little thing was, mated.

She released her hold on my neck, licking at the wounds like a cat. She rolled to the side and out from between my legs. I ached at the loss of contact.

"Remove your clothing." Her eyes were hooded as she watched me. The white of her fangs glinted as she licked her lips.

My hands shook as I moved to do as she asked. I felt weak and feverish. How could my need for her be making me physically ill? It took some work to remove my soaked shoes and jeans, the material clinging to my body. I didn't wear anything under my jeans, so after removing them and my shirt, I was bare in front of her. My pulsing erection made the extent of my desire fully known.

She moved back toward me, shimmying her way between my legs again with a little help from me. I sighed in relief as soon as our skin touched again. My shaking eased as I wrapped my arms around her body.

"Come into the water with me, Kye." She hummed the words against my lips.

I should have questioned how she knew my name. Red flags should have waved like crazy at the idea of getting into the water with a fanged Siren who had already proved she liked human sushi. I was having a hard time keeping it straight in my mind that this was a dream. It felt far too real. In the end, it didn't really matter whether it was real life or a dream; I would follow her into the water without question.

The end of her tail and her fluke was still hidden in the small hole in the cave's center. I assumed that was the water she wanted me to enter. Refusing to release my hold on her, I half-scooted half-shuffled my way to the edge of the hole. My legs were submerged up to my knees, and her body dangled from my arms.

"You have to release me, handsome."

Reluctantly, I loosened my grip and let her slide down my body and into the pool. She stopped herself right at my hips and nuzzled my thigh. Her head moved nearer to my aching member. If she touched it, I was going to explode.

She licked up my shaft, and my vision shifted as blackness threatened to swallow me. This was not the time to pass out or wake up. Her teeth sank gently into my most prized body part, and again that all-consuming lust tore through my body, ripping away at my humanity. My erection grew hotter, my blood turned to lava by her bite. I had to be dreaming because my erection swelled and ached as it stretched. Nothing crazy dramatic, it was more like I had never been fully erect in the past, and additional blood now pumped into it making my muscles swell and pushing me to a fuller erection.

Licking the tiny prick marks, she slipped into the water. I wasted no time in joining her. The cool water was a welcome relief to my feverish body and aching muscles. The moment I was in the water, she pressed her body against the length of mine.

"Stop trying to swim. Just hold me close." Her words felt

like a caress, and my body obeyed her instantly. It was no wonder there were countless stories about Sirens luring men to their death.

With the added length of her tail, she was much longer than me. As I held her against me and stopped treading water, my body floated with perfect buoyancy. Her beautiful face held no signs of strain, and I was reminded again that I was in her territory now. We swayed as her tail undulated in lazy motions, keeping our heads above water. Each time her tail moved, it would rock against my erection, continuing to build my need past the point I thought possible.

I felt her shudder against my chest, and I wondered if the friction was as innocent as it seemed, or if it was affecting her just as much.

"What's your name, beautiful?" I was about to make love to the girl of my dreams, literally. It wasn't just my body that was being affected by her, my heart was too. I wanted her more than anything I had ever wanted before, and I wanted to have her for the rest of my life. This was more than lust—I wanted to know the name of the woman I would give up my entire world for.

She paused from licking and nipping my chest. "Zosime."

She pronounced Zo, like Joe. Her name sounded like 'zo-see-mae.'

"Zosi. I like it." Smiling, I nipped at her earlobe.

"Zosi?"

"Yes, like Josie. A girl's nickname."

She stiffened and then stunned me with a growl. It was a sound I had never heard before. It was a cross between a wolf's growl, a jaguar's hiss, and a creepy alien sound from a horror movie. She pushed away from me.

"This Josie, she is bonded to you?"

Was I imagining it, or had her fangs grown longer? That wasn't possible. I think. We bobbed, water washing over my head. She was twitching her tail like an irritated cat. I wanted to laugh at the absurdity, but I was currently in the water, butt naked, and at the mercy of an angry fanged mermaid.

"No! Josie is a common female name. One of my commanders had a wife with that name."

She continued to glare at me through slitted eyes, not bothering to hide her fangs. Water washed over my head, forcing me to begin treading water. The water stirred violently, her tail stirring it up.

"What...what does 'bonded' mean?" I asked between spitting out mouthfuls of saltwater.

The tightness around her eyes eased slightly, and although her tail continued to churn the water around us, the movements were less erratic.

"Among my kind, bonded is a covenant between two people to become mates for life."

"Oh! Like marriage!"

She tilted her head, considering my words. As stupid as it sounds, I could have sworn she was downloading information or talking to someone telepathically.

"Yes. That word is the closest in meaning to my people's word for bonding."

"Then no. I am not bonded, and I have never been bonded." I huffed a laugh. "I haven't ever wanted to be bonded.

Not until tonight. Until you." I couldn't believe the words tumbling out of my mouth, perhaps it was because this was just a dream. But that didn't change the fact that every single word was true. I would bond to her that very night if given the chance. I imagined someone officiating a ceremony from the side of the cave to marry a naked man and a mermaid, and chuckled.

Zosi floated back up against me. I wrapped my arms around her and relaxed as she took over swimming for both of us.

"You would bond with me tonight?" Her sultry voice sent goosebumps across my skin.

"Without question. I'd love nothing more than to bond with you tonight."

"Okay." She smiled and moved up to capture my lips. This taste of honey and salt danced across my tongue, and just as before, my body instantly flared to life. The effects from our previous make-out session hadn't worn off, and I had been growing more tired with each minute that passed. When she had pulled away, the symptoms became worse. I could think of nothing but sinking inside her and claiming her as mine.

Now.

CHAPTER SEVEN

ZOSIME

T he things this man was doing to my body shouldn't be possible. My emotions were bound by the Ancients, and only they were able to undo it. Yet the stone encasing my heart had begun to fracture just being near these men. With Kye's hands and lips on my body, the walls had started to crumble, and pieces of my emotions slipped through unchecked.

It was utter chaos inside me. Atlantean, warrior and Siren all struggled against each other. Each nature trying to push forward and gain control. I fought against my inner turmoil, determined to have this time with Kye. I wasn't sure how long my control would last, so I needed to make every moment count.

My immense relief at knowing he was not bonded

surprised me, but the bigger shock came when he said that if it were possible, he would bond with me that night. His thoughts were jumbled, so I couldn't understand every sentence, but those words were crystal clear, and he meant them. The turmoil inside me stilled instantly, the abrupt silence deafening.

That's when it happened. The three sides of me decided in that moment to become one. I had been able to use one or two aspects of my nature at the same time, but never all three. We weren't prepared, but that made no difference. The Atlantean had found her forever love, the Siren had found her delicious mate, and the warrior had found her perfect partner. The fractured parts of me were in agreement for this small window of time.

I wrapped my arms around his neck, pressing our bodies together. Water twirled around us in a sensual dance and our mouths joined in the motion of the dance. Kye grew impossibly harder, and his kisses turned from gentle to hungry. I had a sneaking suspicion of why that might be, but I would have to explore that line of thought later.

Kye's manhood pressed against the apex of my thighs. Yes, my sex was in approximately the same area as it would be on a woman with legs. My skin tingled and burned, and I couldn't wait any longer to feel his touch inside me. I slid my hand down until I touched the most sensitive scales. While all my scales were just as sensitive as my skin, the scales in this area were extraordinarily so. Using two fingers, I pushed aside the scales on either side of my most private spot. The tiny, scaled lips blended seamlessly with the rest of my scales, hiding my sex completely.

My finger slipped inside the heated channel, ensuring I was well lubricated. I needn't have worried. Moving my other hand away from his neck, I maneuvered it between us until I could wrap my fingers around his thick erection. Kye gave an involuntary jerk and groaned into my mouth.

His unexpected lurch caused me to again nick his lip. The delicious spicy taste of his blood exploded in my mouth. Nothing had tasted this amazing since I had awakened. I was forced to drink blood to survive. The taste didn't repulse me, but it was more about survival than savoring a meal. It had been a challenge to pull back the first time I tasted Kye's blood. I needed him. His body, his blood, and his love.

Kye's hips jerked, his heavy erection moving in my hand as he sought relief. No more waiting, we had a lifetime to explore each other's bodies. Moving away from his mouth, I sank my fangs into his neck. At the same moment I lined him up with my slit and with a flick of my fluke, I sheathed him inside me in one hard thrust. Our bodies slammed against each other; his hot member buried as far as it could go.

My eyes rolled back in my head and for a moment I thought I might pass out. There was a sharp pain as he stretched me past the point that was comfortable. I hadn't given myself time to adjust to his size slowly in my eagerness to have him in me. To my surprise, the edge of pain aroused me even more and I teetered on the edge of my release.

Kye must have experienced similar sensations. When his pulsing erection had been shoved inside me, slamming against my walls, he had growled through clenched teeth. He grasped me tightly against him, his chest shuddering with each breath he sucked into his lungs.

"Don't move. If you move, I will lose it. Give me a minute, please." His teeth were still clenched. "You are so tight, Zosi. So tight."

His voice sounded pained, and I worried I had hurt him. I released his neck to say, "Are you injured?"

"No, nothing like that. I've never felt anything this good."

I said nothing, instead sinking my teeth back into his neck, unable to resist the aromatic scent of his blood that made my mouth water. I felt his body pulse inside me in response to the bite.

Gradually his grip eased, and I took that as my cue that he had regained control. I began to undulate my tail in the water, my pace unhurried. The motion moved him in and out of me. The feeling of him rubbing along my walls had me growling against his skin. I tried to go slow, but the Siren could wait no longer. The water around us had continued to swirl, but now it sloshed and splashed as my pace grew faster. The rocking undulation of my fin had Kye's member thrusting in and out of me. Each time he sheathed himself, our groins banged together.

Kye never tried to take over, instead he gripped my hips and allowed my tail to rush us toward our release. His fingers dug into my hips as I moved us faster and faster. Our breathing was little more than small panting gasps. Kye kept his head tilted to the side so I could continue to drink from him.

58

Stars glittered in my vision, and my stomach clenched. With two more hard slips of my fluke, the coil inside me sprung free and my orgasm crashed over me. My body shook as wave after wave of pleasure rocked through me. Kye shouted my name, his body stiffening as he followed me over the precipice. I could feel his erection pulse as the evidence of release filled me. The feeling of his body jerking inside my tight walls sent another orgasm shuddering through me. I screamed his name in surprise and dug my nails into his skin as I clung to him.

Mine.

He was mine. Forever and always.

I pressed my hand against his heart and my mouth to the spot where I had bitten him. For a moment I stayed still, savoring this moment as we became one. I was no longer alone in the world. I still had so much to figure out, but I would not face it alone. Pulling away, I watched the magik swirl along his skin. It should have been the gold of the Atlanteans, but instead it was the color of my glowing scales. The magik etched a shimmering tattoo from the skin above his heart, up to his shoulder, and finally connecting with the imprint of my teeth. The bite mark was incorporated into the intricate design, not hidden, but a part of the tattoo.

"Αν έπρεπε να ζήσω τη ζωή μου ξανά, θα σε έβρισκα νωρίτερα."

I met Kye's startled gaze. "I understood you," he whispered. "You said, 'If I were to live my life again, I'd find you sooner.' How am I able to understand you?"

"Because we are one. You are mine, and I am yours."

59

I kissed the full lips of my handsome mate, ready to find more ways to enjoy each other's bodies. I felt the answering stir of his body still inside me. This was going to be a deliciously long night.

Suddenly, the sound of shouting ricocheted around the cave. There were no entrances to the little cave, the only way to get it was to go through the underwater tunnel. The chamber was about sixteen by twelve feet. It was dry, although water sloshed onto the dark rough stones around the mouth of the tunnel. The ceiling was almost solid rock, patches of velvet black sky and stars could be seen through small holes, and it also allowed us to hear some of the sounds from the outside world.

I stilled against the hard muscled planes of Kye's body and my instincts kicked into overdrive. Emotions were trying to break through the magik barriers that held them back. I had just bonded with my mate, and that left me feeling raw. Atlanteans disappeared from society for several months after bonding. This allowed them to focus on the needs and desires of their claimed mate. It also gave both partners time to adjust to the physical and mental changes that came from an Atlantean bonding. I hadn't had time to explain things to Kye, things that ideally, he should have been told before I sealed our bond.

What I was having more trouble controlling was the feral nature of the Siren. I had grown up as an Atlantean, but I had barely begun to understand the changes that had happened to my body as the ocean swallowed Atlantis. The changes to my body were obvious, but the mental differences and instincts were unfamiliar and less predictable. The second row of teeth dropped down behind the first. My mouth tingled and I tasted the sweet taste of toxin. That had been a shock, one more ability that had manifested when the need arose.

Voices grew louder, carrying across the water. They wanted my mate. He was going to be taken from me. I couldn't go with him unless I wanted to risk being captured. For a moment I thought about dragging them all beneath the waves, then they wouldn't be able to take Kye from me. But recognizing the voices as belonging to his friends on the boat, Storm, Eason, and Fynn, I knew it would be impossible to harm them. They were mine too, although I didn't know how Kye would take that. We had much to discuss and learn about each other.

Atlantis had very open ideas regarding love, and relationships of all types were common. It was not uncommon for there to be several people in one relationship. From the thoughts I had picked up from the humans of this time, multiple partners in a single relationship was less accepted and often considered strange. I would honor his wishes, but I hoped that Kye would consider the ways of my kind.

"Zosi, my love," Kye whispered gently. "My friends are worried, I need to go to them. I don't want to this dream to end, but this may be my call to wake up." He pulled himself from my slick folds. Our bodies were still aroused, and the friction sent a shudder through both of us.

What did he want to wake up from? He wasn't asleep. I focused and his thoughts swirled in my mind. There were memories that seemed to come from a dream—mating with a mermaid, our bodies moving together like an erotic dream, moments when he thought of waking. It was confusing, and the thoughts blended into each other.

"You are not asleep. Stay with me." I could barely hear my own words.

"Oh, how I wish I could, my love. I know a day will never pass without me thinking of this perfect dream, and my incredible dream girl." His lips pressed against my hair, and he inhaled in my scent. He was trying to commit everything about me to memory.

My eyes burned, but I did not cry. I had never heard of anyone leaving their mate the day they had consummated the bond. These hours were important, but I would not force Kye to remain with me. I would take him to the others; I would do anything for him. He carried a piece of my soul now.

"I will take you," I said. "Even with equipment, a human would struggle to navigate this tunnel. You must breathe slowly and lower your heart rate. When you need air, expel your air fully and seal your lips against mine."

Curiosity stirred in Kye's eyes when he looked back at me. "Don't you need that air? I don't want you to pass out!"

Laughter tried to bubble up inside me, but the barriers continued to force it back. I was surprised to find that I wanted to remember what it felt like to laugh. "I breathe beneath the water. Now, get dressed. if you are truly leaving, we need to go soon."

Kye struggled into his clothes, snagging them. Once he was ready, he turned to look at me.

"Focus your breathing," I told him as I moved toward him.

Nodding his head, he closed his eyes and focused on his breathing. I did the same. I had not told him the challenge this would pose for me. I needed to allow one lung to fill with water, while letting the other remain full of air. If I were human, that level of control wouldn't be possible. However, just because I could do it, didn't mean it was easy. I had practiced this only a few times and each time it was painful, not unlike drowning. But Kye didn't need to know that this was the only way to get him safely from the cave without alerting outsiders to my hidden home.

Propelling myself higher in the water, I captured Kye's lips in my own. I poured what emotions I was capable of into those precious seconds.

"Breath deep." I watched him pack air into his lungs. With a small dip of his chin, he signaled that he was ready.

"Θα σε αγαπάω για πάντα."

His eyes widened but I didn't give him time to respond before dragging him into the obsidian waters of the tunnel. I had traveled this route many times before, and I avoided the jagged rocks that jutted from the walls with ease. My scales pulsed their blue-green light, casting a soft glow around us. The tunnel went deep into the earth before taking a sharp curve up and opening into waters near mouth of the bay. The boat was not far from my cave if you had the wings of a bird, but the maze beneath the ocean took longer to navigate.

We were nearing the steep bend when Kye released a curtain of bubbles and pressed his lip against mine. For a moment, I wanted to pause and savor his lips, but I did not have enough air in my lung for long delays. I opened my mouth against his, my muscles constricting painfully as I sealed the water-filled lung and opened the pipe to my air-filled lung. He drew in what he needed, and then pulled away. His lips lingered against mine for mere second. I reversed the process in my chest, gritting my teeth against the discomfort.

Our surroundings were little more than a blur as my powerful fluke propelled us forward. We streaked into the ocean, and I turned and headed straight for the vessel. The shouts of the men could be heard even beneath the waves. Large spotlights shined on the water; they were using everything they could to locate Kye. I slowed to dodge the blinding lights. Kye's lips pressed against my lips once more, and again I gave him air. This time, I allowed both lungs to fill with water. That first long breath of cool saltwater eased the burn in my chest. I took several breaths in a row, moving faster now that I was no longer functioning on a single lung.

Kye's arms tightened painfully around my waist when I swam deeper. I would not risk being seen. Once we were directly beneath the boat, I began our ascent to the surface. The outline of the back of the boat came into view. When we were six feet from the surface, I halted our forward motion. Kye's questioning look made it clear that he expected me to surface alongside him.

Shaking my head, I wiggled free of his snug embrace. He had already begun to float toward the surface, and I used my newly discovered water abilities to move him the last few feet to the surface. He struggled to reach for me, but I turned and sank into the depths. I lurked beneath the boat until I saw his legs disappear as his friends pulled him from the dark sea. Once he was safe, I made my escape.

I headed straight for the ocean. The shallow water surrounding the bay wasn't going to be safe with the humans looking for me. I needed to hide from them, but I also wanted to escape my hurt. For a beautiful moment, I had thought I wouldn't have to be alone anymore.

Swimming into the black depths of the sea, I realized I had never felt so alone in my entire existence.

CHAPTER EIGHT

KYE

I broke the surface and gasped in the salty warm air. I had fully expected to wake up from unconsciousness when I surfaced. Instead, Eason and Storm shouted exclamations and hauled me from the water. Fynn stepped forward, a thick towel held out toward me. I thanked him and grabbed the towel. I wiped at the salt water that was burning my nose.

"Where have you been? How did you escape?" Fynn spoke first.

"Escape? From what?" I replied.

"The mermaid that surfaced with you in her arms," Fynn almost shouted back. "She told us you were alive, and that she wouldn't hurt you. Then she warned us not to get in the water because a shark was nearby. It's highly likely that *she* is the one responsible for the climbing body count. We worried you were her next victim." His words came out like a torrent, his fear and anxiety apparent.

"She wouldn't do that!" I said it with confidence, but the reality was I had no way of knowing if it was true or not. After we made love, something inside me shifted and I had thought I could feel her. I couldn't clearly read her thoughts, but there was a ghostly impression of them. It had been just another intriguing twist of the illusion.

"Did she tell you that?" Eason's snort of derision had me snapping my head up to lock eyes with him.

"No, we didn't talk about it. She was—" How was I supposed to describe her?

"Kye, I am sure any of us would fall in love with a mermaid that rescued us, but remember that she is a predator," Storm said. "From the little I saw, she is literally built to kill. We were helpless to stop her tonight and that was terrifying." Storm's tone wasn't condescending, and I knew where he was coming from. They were all wrong, though.

"It's a dream. I'll wake up any minute." I closed my eyes tightly, praying that I would wake up and none of this would be real. The most incredible dream of my life was fast becoming a nightmare. Just the thought that this might not be a dream had bile rising up my throat. I was the one who asked to cut our time together short, and I had let her swim away. Her last words to me had been in Greek, but my mind had understood her meaning, even though I knew nothing about the language.

I will love you forever.

Those were the last words she said to me. I hadn't even had a chance to respond before she pulled us underwater. If this was all real, then I had let the love of my life slip through my hands like water and she didn't even know that I loved her too.

Groaning, I dropped onto the deck with a thud and pressed my face into the damp towel. Storm eased down on one side of me, and Fynn settled on the other side.

"What's going on, little brother?" Storm wasn't my brother, none of us were related by blood, but that didn't change the depth of our relationship.

Heaving a sigh, I recounted the entire saga. I did, however, skim over the details of our lovemaking. "How can I be sure I'm not still asleep?" I moaned in frustration.

Suddenly, a fist connected with my stomach, hard enough to knock the wind from me, but not hard enough to truly hurt me. "What the heck, Eason?"

"I was just proving you were awake." His casual shrug was irritating.

"You couldn't just pinch me like a normal person?" I growled.

"That's for wimps."

I wanted to wipe the smug smirk off his face, but I was exhausted and heartsick. I wanted to sleep for the next week straight, but I also wanted to jump in the ocean and find Zosi.

Fynn spoke, his voice coming from far away. "He's going into shock. Our questions will have to wait until he has been rested and checked for injuries." His hands moved along my skin feeling for my pulse and temperature. My eyelids turned to lead, drooping with the weight. Unable to bear the heartache of losing her, I let unconsciousness steal me away.

CHAPTER NINE

FYNN

Kye's body went slack, and he slumped against me. "Guys, we really need to get him back to shore and to a hospital," I said.

"No hospitals, not yet anyway," Storm replied firmly. "We can't explain what happened, which means they won't be able to help him. If she bit him and released venom, the hospitals won't have an anti-venom for that, since Sirens aren't real. We'll get him back to our room and you can examine him there. If you believe there are internal injuries, we will take him for X-rays at the medical examiner's office. If those show internal injuries that require surgery or medical supplies outside of what we can obtain, *then* we will make the trip to the hospital."

Storm's tone made it clear this wasn't up for debate. I

understood his decision, but I didn't have to like it. Growing up, books were my friends and they had opened doors to things I had found fascinating. As an adult, I was still a loner, never fitting in with those around me. Even when undertaking my research work, I preferred my home office or visiting the lab after hours to work. I filled the long hours alone by studying, and I had earned degrees in several fields. One of those was a PhD, although I had never practiced as a doctor after finishing my residency. I would have preferred a doctor check him over at a hospital immediately. If there was a problem, the delay could cost Kye his life.

Eason turned the boat back toward the shore, careful to stay just inside the posted speed limits. Storm pulled Kye against him to keep Kye's limp frame from banging against the boat. There was nothing romantic between these three men. Their shared bond was that of brothers, not by blood, but by choice. They were family, and I longed to have that for myself.

In under thirty minutes we were settling Kye on his bed. Eason and Storm stepped to the side, close enough to observe, but far enough to give me space to move around him without feeling cramped.

I started with his head, wanting to check the spot that had impacted with the boat. "That's weird, there should be a lump and a cut here. We know he was knocked unconscious and there was blood on the boat and in the water, but there are no signs of an injury. That isn't possible." I checked again, and then stepped aside as Storm looked for the point of impact as well. There wasn't so much as a lump or papercut to mark the spot. He stepped back, shaking his head in confusion.

"Let's remove his shirt." With a few grunts as we lifted and maneuvered his dead weight, we managed to get it off. As his shoulder came into view, I gasped.

"Has he always had this tattoo?"

"What tattoo? He doesn't have..." Eason's words trailed off as he stared at the markings that traveled down Kye's neck to his shoulder and then lower toward his heart. The design was elegant, reminding me of the swirling sea. The lines were glowing, aquamarine light ebbing and flowing throughout the tattoo. Letters of an alphabet I didn't recognize spelled something about his heart. This type of art piece would have taken days to complete, but somehow it had been done in two or three hours. One more impossibility to add to our growing list.

"What's that on his neck?" Storm pointed to a spot where the design created a beautiful circular seal, the type often used by royalty. In the middle of the circle there were additional words in that unfamiliar script, and a—"Bite mark. He's been bitten!"

Utter panic ensued.

I scrambled to check his vitals for the umpteenth time. Eason grabbed his keys and started putting his shoes on the wrong feet. Storm grabbed his phone and made the motions to call someone but couldn't decide who. I'm not sure what would have happened if Kye hadn't decided to wake up in the middle of our chaos.

"Ugh. Guys? What is going on?" He rubbed at his temple

73

and tried to sit up. His body trembled with the effort. With a groan he collapsed back on the bed.

"We will get you to the hospital. Just hang in there, Kye!" Storm couldn't hide the fear in his voice.

"I'm tired, not dying. Chill." Kye huffed a breathless laugh that helped to reassure all of us that he wasn't truly dying.

"Kye, do you remember being bitten? How long ago did it happen?" I peered into his eyes checking for discoloration.

To my shock, he blushed. "Fynn, I like you a lot, but back up a bit." He was trying to distract me.

"So, you do remember being bitten," I said. "Why did she bite you? Have there been any side effects or symptoms?"

Kye turned a deeper shade of crimson. Roars of laughter startled me, and I jumped. Eason and Storm collapsed into chairs and laughed until tears streamed down their faces. "What's so funny? Kye's life may still be in danger!"

The men tried to speak, but between their gasps for air and raucous laughter, I couldn't make sense of it.

"She bit me while we were being intimate," Kye said with a sigh. "Those jerks figured it out. I'm not going to die from it. It did have, um, side effects, but she fixed that." He wouldn't even look at me as he spoke, and his skin remained red.

"Side effects like what? I need specifics to figure out what we are dealing with." I grabbed my pen and paper, preparing to make notes that we could use later if needed.

Kye's eyes finally met mine and he looked horrified. "You're going to write it down?" His voice cracked in panic.

I looked in confusion at Eason and Storm, but they had been set off into another round of laughter. I wasn't sure how we were supposed to get to the bottom of this if everyone kept acting like children. Clicking my pen over and over, a habit I had developed as a kid, I waited for everyone to calm down. It took about ten minutes for the guys to get ahold of themselves, wipe their eyes, and stop chuckling.

"Fynn, you really need to relax a bit," Storm said with a grin. "I always thought Eason was uptight, but you have him beat." Storm's smile made it clear this was playful banter; he was not belittling me.

"You aren't the first to say that." I sighed. These guys were the first men I had ever felt like I belonged with. It made zero sense considering how long we had known each other. My heart said they were my tribe, even as my mind said that was sentimental and ridiculous.

Eason walked over and slapped me on the back. "Give us time, we'll make you unwind." He turned toward Kye. "Alright kid, you left out a lot of details on the boat when you described your encounter with the mermaid. I don't care if it's embarrassing. It's time to tell us everything."

Kye's shoulder sagged. Taking a deep breath, he began to tell the story again, except this time when he got to the part about their intimacy, he retold it in great detail. I forgot to write; my pen frozen on the paper as he described the encounter. Never in my life had I heard anything this erotic. A hard bulge formed in my pants, and I moved my notebook to cover it, embarrassed that the guys might have noticed it.

When Kye finished speaking, he adjusted his pants and cleared his throat a few times. Eason threw a bottle of water at him but didn't bother to get up. I hid my smile; it turns out I wasn't the only one affected by the tale.

Storm spoke up, his voice low and rough, "It sounds like she managed to counteract her venom. It's good to know that there's a cure, or an antivenom. Maybe it's her saliva? Perhaps she's the cure for her venom."

I choked on my own laughter. Now it was their turn to watch me with irritated gazes as I howled. With herculean effort I managed to speak, "Oh yes, she is definitely the cure!" It took several more minutes for me to pull myself together.

"Care to elaborate, Doctor?" Eason raised his brow, impatience showing in his squinted eyes.

"Yes, yes," I said, collecting myself. "Okay, it sounds like she can control her venom. Based on Kye's symptoms, her venom acted as an aphrodisiac. Maybe a smaller dose has these effects, while a larger dose is lethal. I would need to study that more to be sure. However, what we do know is that it worked as a sexual stimulant in Kye. He was experiencing health issues, until they completed copulation—"

"Did he just say 'copulation?'" Kye's eyes were wide, and his mouth hung open in horror.

"Do you prefer coitus?" I queried.

Eason snorted.

"Coupling? Intercourse? Fornicati—"

Storm broke in. "Sex. You are saying that she injected him with a stimulant to ensure he would perform. What would be the point? Maybe she needed a male to procreate?"

Kye looked faint, his skin turning a sickly green shade.

Eason's eyes glinted in humor. "Did you hear that, Kye?

She basically gave you the mermaid's version of a little blue pill."

"It wasn't like that!" Kye cried. "I was already aroused before she bit me, and I came onto her first. We both wanted it and consented to it verbally." He paused and rubbed his eyes.

"Fynn may be right about its affects, though," he confessed. "It didn't force me to be aroused, but it definitely enhanced our lovemaking."

"It would be very interesting to study the effects in person," I added.

All three guys guffawed. My cheeks grew warm from embarrassment.

"Purely for science! I didn't mean it like that!"

They snickered and elbowed each other like they were thirteen years old instead of in their twenties and early thirties.

"Fine, it sounded weird," I conceded. "From what Kye said, the flu-like symptoms of the toxin eased, but didn't cease completely. That might be why he's still shaky." I sighed and turned to Kye. "I wish we had a sample to study. We still don't know why your injuries healed, or how she gave you an intricate tattoo in minutes. If I weren't looking at the evidence, I wouldn't believe it. I wish we could read that language. Maybe I could send some photos to my friends and see if they recognize the script."

"I want to see it, is there a mirror?" Kye glanced around the room. Flicking the blanket off his body he prepared to stand.

"Stay in bed!" I barked. Moving toward him, I pulled out

my cell phone and snapped a photo. I handed him the phone, watching his face as he zoomed in on the script. He unconsciously moved his mouth as he studied the photograph. Color drained from his face and the phone trembled in his hand.

"What is it? Why do you look like someone died?" Storm asked what we were all wondering.

Kye moved his hand up and rubbed the tattoo. When he finally met our eyes, I saw the tears in his own. "We bonded, and I left her."

"Bonded? What does that mean?"

My stomach dropped. Eason may not understand, but I believed I knew what Kye was saying. "Are you sure?" I asked him.

"Yes." His voice was barely a whisper. "I can't read the words, but somehow I know what they symbolize. She asked, and I agreed. I believed it was a dream. The thing is, even if I had known it was real, I still would have said yes. I can't explain it because it doesn't make sense. But I knew she was mine and I was hers. Nothing else mattered."

"Is someone going to explain what on earth he's talking about?" Eason asked.

I turned to face Eason.

"I'm guessing there's a lot more at play here judging by her effect on him and the magical tattoos," I said. "But the short answer is, he got married tonight, got his rocks off, and then ditched his new bride."

CHAPTER TEN

ZOSIME

I spent six days hidden in the depths. The obsidian darkness that had once bothered me, now enveloped me in a way that made me feel secure. I lay curled on the sandy bed of the ocean floor. My scales remained dark, not bothering to light the world around me, a world I didn't care to see.

Even when I had held my emotions centuries ago, I would never have been this devastated. I was chosen to be one of the Promised because of my warrior heart. Being soft was nothing to be ashamed of, but it wasn't me. I was the one who helped to protect the tenderhearted. Now I hid in the darkness, nursing a broken heart. Idly, I wondered how I would have survived this devastation if my emotions weren't still being partially blocked.

It seemed impossible that a stranger could affect me so

much. It had to be the instant bonding. Hot salty tears mixed with the cool saltwater around me. I had no one to ask about the bonding legends, and I doubted any scrolls from Atlantis had survived in the collapse. Maybe it was time for me to return to the waters of my childhood and search for any ruins of my home and her people.

Rough skin slid against my own, startling me out of my own little 'pity party.' That was a term I heard in the mind of the female but didn't understand until Kye had climbed onto that boat and left me behind. Rousing myself, I thought of my shimmering scales and slowly they flickered to life. A wave of dizziness washed over me the moment I pushed myself into a sitting position. It wasn't until that moment that I realized how weak I felt. I had gone too long without eating.

Dim green light lit the waters a few feet around me. It was just enough to see the massive grey and white body not four feet from my face. I flattened myself into the sand and silt, gritting my teeth as her rough skin rubbed against the length of my body. It was the same impressive shark that had been lurking around me since I swam into these waters.

I watched as she turned and moved toward me again. The sheer size and girth of her body made her turns a bit slower. This time as she neared me, I pushed at her head, using the force to propel me backwards and away from her.

"Why won't you leave me alone!"

There wasn't an answer, not that I expected one. This female had found me in the depths and shoved at me until I would get up and begin swimming. I would find another spot, only to have her find me the next day and repeat her annoying ritual. It reminded me of the Atlanteans who had tamed wild dogs and kept them inside their homes. The dogs would beg for food, to be petted, and to play outdoors. They were as demanding as children! Secretly, I had always wished for a hound as well, but my life had been dedicated to serving Atlantis and that wouldn't have been fair to an animal.

Now I found myself being followed around by an eighteen-foot shark who acted like one of the small hounds from my memories. Just like everything else in my life, it was disconcerting and made no sense. She glided past me again, much slower this time. I ran my hands down her smokey-colored sides and pearl-colored stomach. Satisfied that I was awake, she moved away, disappearing into the gloom around me. With a sigh, I started my own journey toward land. If I didn't want to die, I needed to find food. It was time I headed back to my homeland, and swimming the length of an entire ocean would require strength.

I HAD MADE IT ONLY A COUPLE OF MILES BEFORE THE call began. The Lure was nearby, and I was needed. The good news was that a meal had just presented itself, the bad news was that I was weakened, and this would be a harder kill if the human was fit and healthy.

I tried to pick up my pace, but my movements remained sluggish. I had snacked on a few fish, which provided small amounts of nutrients, but my new form also required blood in larger amounts than was provided by the tiny fish. What I had taken from Kye should have lasted for several more days. My guess was the binding magik had depleted my body, and since I hadn't taken blood after leaving him, I was suffering from starvation.

Humans could go much longer without food, especially if they had access to fresh water. I was learning about this new body through trial and error, and I had noticed that the cooler water used my energy reserves faster than warm water. This meant that as long as I stayed in the warm waters, I could go longer between blood feedings. Small fish that I caught could give me a tiny boost to last an extra day or two. Between my exhaustion after the binding, the amount of time since I drank from anyone, and the cooler temperatures of the deeps where I had been resting, this was the worst shape I had been in since waking.

There was also a strange throbbing in my chest I hadn't felt before. I guessed it had something to do with Kye, but I didn't know if it was the pain of him leaving me, or if being separated from one's mate was the cause. Anything was possible when Ancient magik was involved. The theory would be tested when I began my journey across the sea and the distance between us grew larger.

The ocean around me turned from pitch black to midnight blue, then to a soft blue as the light penetrated the shallow water. I enjoyed the feel of the silky warm waters caressing my body, but I also felt exposed. The tropical waters in the gulf were clear in most areas, so someone standing on a boat and looking down would be able to see me, or at least see my dark outline. The sooner I answered the call and headed back into the depths, the better.

The vibrations of the boat's idling motor reached me first, with the man's thoughts blasting into my mind moments later. He was thinking of the things he had done to a young waitress the night before, things that made acidic bile make its way up my throat. She wasn't the first he had brutalized, nor did he plan for her to be the last.

My skin crawled and to my astonishment, liquid anger burned through me. I answered the call, but I did not get emotional over it. Disgusted, yes. But anger was one of the emotions that had been buried. It was a messy emotion that simply got in the way of our job, just like pity, sadness, and guilt. This was not good.

I moved faster toward the boat, my fury lending me a small burst of energy that I would pay for later. Both sets of fangs dropped into place and I could taste the toxin in my mouth. I wished I had better control over the venom, I didn't want this man to die quickly, I wanted him to suffer. See? This is exactly why anger is an issue when you're a warrior. He needed to die, it shouldn't matter to me if his death was fast or slow, only that it was efficient.

His slimy thoughts in my mind stoked my anger into a volcanic rage. I wanted him to suffer like he had forced his victims to suffer. Some of the women had been left alive to relive their trauma over and over in their minds while they tried to rebuild their lives. Others had been killed and their bodies were scattered around the island in shallow graves. Nausea churned in my stomach. I would have to speak to someone on land before I left this place. Those girls deserved to be found, and their families deserved to bury their loved ones. Pushing those worries aside, I focused back on the boat I was circling.

Annoyance. The emotion echoed in my mind, yanking it back from the dark feral place it had been heading. It was a strange feeling to feel an emotion so strongly, but know it wasn't yours. It wasn't coming from the filth above me either; I sensed his emotions, but I didn't feel them, nor did I feel anyone else's emotions. I was far too exhausted to deal with this. Moving closer, I suctioned my palms against the side of the boat, edging myself nearer to my victim.

Worry. Again, an emotion that didn't belong to me washed through my mind, and made my heart skip a beat. I grit my teeth, irritated. I was hunting and struggling to maintain control of my own unruly emotions; this wasn't the time or place to deal with someone else's feelings. The man above me was carefree, not a worry in his mind. He had taken what he wanted and had gotten away with it. I ground my jaw so tightly that my fangs pierced my lip in several places.

Focus. Let the call wash away everything but the mission.

It didn't work. I was hungry and angry. What did the female with the knives call this? Oh yes, she called it being *hangry.* A fitting name for this state of being. Reaching out, I yanked hard on the man's fishing line. He let loose with a string of curses and his feet stumbled on the deck. The boat tilted slightly as he leaned over the edge to peer into the water, no doubt trying to see what he had caught on his line.

I was tired and knew I couldn't waste this opportunity.

Using everything in me, I propelled myself up and onto his body. Sinking my hands into his shirt, I pulled him from the safety of his small fishing vessel and into the waters with me. The predator in me uncoiled, pleased with her catch. We sank beneath the surface. His struggles made little difference to me; in the water, I was stronger than he could imagine. I was not one of the helpless young women he enjoyed preying on. The hunter was now the hunted.

Shock. I gasped as the new emotion battered my mind. My heart began to race, experiencing another emotion that didn't belong to me. I struggled to focus on the task at hand, but the damage had already been done. Sharp pain sliced between my ribs. Glancing down, I stared at the small knife that the man had embedded in the softer skin of my side. He shoved at my body, a nasty smirk on his lips.

I flashed my fangs at him in a feral smile. The pain had startled me and that had been enough for me to lose control over the turmoil inside me. The Siren had come out to play. His skin paled to a deathly shade as he took in my fangs and slitted eyes. He was looking death in the face, and he knew it.

Moving forward, my fangs sank savagely into the vein on his neck. The blood tasted like water from a wishing well filled with old coins. Basically, it tasted nasty. This had never truly bothered me until I had drunk from Kye. I drank to survive; it didn't matter if I enjoyed it or not. Now I knew that it could be pleasurable and taste better than any food I had ever enjoyed in my life. That knowledge made it much more difficult to choke down the foul taste of this man's blood.

My claws extended and sank into his shoulders; he would

not escape my grip. I was careful to not inject him with venom. The Siren wanted him to suffer, and I couldn't stop her. His blood mixed with my own which poured from my side, and it excited the feral part of me even more. Ripping my fangs from his skin, I released my hold on his neck, turning his neck to bury my fangs deeper on the other side.

Fear. The emotion did not concern me, it was not my own. I felt only the thrill of the hunt.

Panic. Once more, I shoved at the emotion, wanting to enjoy my prey's futile struggles.

Sadness. I froze. There was something familiar...

It hit me with the force of a tsunami. Kye. The emotions belonged to him, and I was feeling them because he was my soulmate. He had to be near for me to be sensing his emotions. I hadn't been able to feel them when I was in the depths. Something was very wrong. He needed me.

I grappled to control the Siren who wasn't finished playing with her meal. She had been careful not to take too much blood right away, not wanting to let him slip immediately into unconsciousness. Unfortunately, that was biting us in the dorsal fin now. I needed to get to Kye, and deal with whatever had put him in danger. He left me, but he was still my mate, and I would always honor our bond.

I sank my fangs into the man one last time and delivered a dose of venom that would have paralyzed a whale. My unique toxin worked fast, and his limbs immediately seized. His face contorted in horrific pain, the toxin freezing the expression on his face like a tribal mask. I released my hold, and he sank toward the ocean floor several feet below. He could see his boat but wouldn't be able to reach it. The Siren despised knowing that he would die in less than a minute, escaping the punishment she had planned for him, but I resisted the urge to go back for more. Twisting around, I shot through the water, following Kye's emotions like a shark seeking blood.

My warrior's mind blocked out the pain in my side and allowed me to focus on what had to be done.

My Atlantean heart pushed me forward, well past my limits, prepared to give everything to save my soulmate.

My Siren's body shifted and changed, eager to destroy anything that dared to threaten what belonged to me.

I'm coming, Kye.

And I was bringing death with me.

CHAPTER ELEVEN

EASON

We had headed out this morning, exactly as we had every other morning the past week. There hadn't been any deaths since the night the mermaid brought Kye back to our boat. We had been sent here to determine and then resolve any threats in this area. Now we knew what, or rather who, had caused the death. But she was nowhere to be seen.

However, thanks to extensive research and calls to Kye's computer genius friends, we had a pretty good idea of the 'why' behind her kills. The sleepy little towns scattered around the bay had a habit 'forgetting' to record certain crimes that were perpetrated by individuals belonging to their oldest families. Those roots ran deep, and some of the officers were turning a blind eye to their crimes out of misplaced loyalty.

They took the stance that what happened in a citizen's home wasn't any of their business, unless the wife came to them to file a report, or the hospital called them with a victim.

There were many wonderful hardworking people in these quaint towns, but some of the guys had started to rub off on each other. The bar fights were loud, and when they were kicked out to 'sober up,' most went home to vent their frustrations on those they swore to love. The men quickly realized that if they kept their women and kids quiet, they wouldn't face any real trouble from the law.

I had wanted to break every piece of furniture in our room when the information had started trickling in. Kye had printed out files for each of the men that his contact sent information on. When the contact had realized the depth of the cover-ups in the area, he had expanded his digging, no longer focusing only on our victims. Reading through file after file, I had wanted to go pay a visit to each of the men and ensure they never lifted another drunk fist to their family members. Yet file after file, I was shocked to find that the mermaid had beat me to it.

By the time we finished sorting the files, we had discovered that some of the men were missing, some were laying on cold steel tables in the morgue, and only three remained alive. She was a highly efficient assassin, and I admired her for it. In a few weeks' time, she had nearly wiped out a hotbed of cruelty, and changed the lives of two dozen women and children.

The single female victim had been more of a mystery, and it took an entire team of computer guys, as well as us doing our own investigations, to figure out what her backstory was. She had been kidnapped, and reading about the things she had endured made me burn in rage. I wanted to slaughter her tormentors, but somehow, she had managed to do it herself. She had gone in, armed with knives, and had exacted her revenge.

What disgusted me most was how the cover up had twisted the story. If she had been taken into custody, she would have faced charges and would have been incarcerated the rest of her life. She had just gotten her freedom and would have been sentenced to live in a cage again. What kind of justice was that? Instead, she had been given a merciful death, and from Fynn's examination, it appeared that she went willingly. I didn't like it, but I could see a weird logic to it.

We suspected that someone high up in law enforcement was behind much of the corruption, but we hadn't been able to figure out who...yet. It was only a matter of time. Finding people was our specialty, and we never missed a target.

Which was probably why we found ourselves in the middle of an absolute crap-storm. First, our air tanks had malfunctioned, leaving us without air shortly after we had started our dive. Thankfully we weren't down too deep, and after years spent in the water gaining longer breath holds, we were able to ascend without risking serious injury. But things only got worse from there.

Storm grabbed the ladder preparing to climb back onto the boat. The moment he put his weight on the bottom rung, the engine exploded. It was a small explosion, designed to cause maximum damage while not being large enough to draw the attention of other boats that could come to our aid.

Kye, Fynn and I were hit by small pieces of debris that sliced through our suits. Storm had taken the brunt of the explosion and was hurled back into the sea. While I had only minor cuts, he had several pieces of fiberglass embedded in his skin. His body hit the water like a limp ragdoll. Kye scrambled to him, keeping his head above water, while Fynn assessed his injuries and tried to staunch the blood flow.

I was the rock in our friendship, the tough guy that feared nothing. But in that moment, my heart seized. We had all suffered wounds to various degrees, and now our blood was turning the water around us red. It was astounding how even a small amount of blood could tint the water such a brilliant shade. If we could see it, any sharks within a quarter mile radius would be able to smell it.

The boat listed to the right, taking on water fast; it would be underwater within minutes. We had no weapons, and no way to get ourselves out of the water. I moved toward the boat, careful to not get trapped in the suction from its sinking. If I could find our duffel, I could use the satellite phone to call for help. I was five feet from the boat when I came across the shredded material of the bag. It had been destroyed, along with everything that had been inside it.

We were miles from shore, a distance we could have easily swam had we been uninjured. I searched the horizon but not a single ship was in sight. Considering the string of deaths recently and law enforcement's warnings to avoid the waters, it wasn't a surprise. Our team had been in tight situations before, but I wasn't sure how we would get out of this.

A brown dorsal fin sliced through the water ten feet from us, quickly followed by a second fin, and then a third. What little bit of hope I was clinging to immediately vanished. These were bull sharks, one of the most dangerous shark species on earth. I didn't fault them for their instincts. We were in their home, and we were injured. They were simply doing what they had been designed to do, and we were ringing the shark equivalent of a dinner bell with our blood. I would still prefer not to be eaten, but I just didn't see a way to avoid it.

Then, a fourth fin broke the surface, joining the others as they circled the debris from the boat that surrounded us. One fin broke away from the others and headed straight at us. The frenzy was about to start. I pushed in front of my brothers.

My role in our group had always been that of protector, even when they didn't know they needed one. I was quiet, preferring to listen than to speak. That had earned me many labels from those outside our team. Cold, cruel, arrogant, egotistical, slow—I had heard them all. I didn't care what strangers thought of me, only that I did my job and did it well. This would be the last time I fought by my brothers' sides, and I would go out doing what made me the happiest. Protecting my family.

The shark turned at the last second, its torpedo-shaped body slamming into me. A second shark moved in, and I barely managed to shove into its way, forcing it to turn. The first shark had circled back around and was moving in fast.

The remaining two sharks had disappeared completely, likely circling beneath us. I felt sick knowing there was no way we could prepare for their attacks. At any moment, one of us could be yanked beneath the waves.

Both sharks were closing in on us, one veering toward Fynn who was frantically applying pressure to a wound on Storm's neck, and the second shark moved toward Kye who was keeping Storm's head above water. Panic made my limbs numb. I couldn't stop both sharks by myself.

But it turned out we weren't alone.

If I hadn't seen it with my own eyes, I never would have believed it. To be honest, I wasn't sure it had really happened.

The sharks were only seconds away from attacking when water exploded into the air in front of us and rained down on our stunned faces. A great white surged up out of the ocean like something off a television drama documentary. The beast had to be nearing twenty feet long, by far the largest living shark I had encountered in the ocean.

I believe I would've had a heart attack on the spot had it not been for the shock of seeing what, or rather who, was clinging to the dorsal fin of the great white. The elusive mermaid was pressed against the shark's side, gripping the dorsal in one hand and a knife in the other. Confidence radiated from her as she held onto one of the world's most terrifying predators as if it were her trusty steed and she was riding it into battle. Dark hair fanned around her face and her glowing eyes quickly assessed our dire situation. She was a breathtakingly stunning warrior. Fury spread across her face, and I wondered who I should fear more—the shark, or this lethal goddess.

I didn't have to wait long to figure it out. She flung herself off the great white, twisting gracefully in the air and slamming into the shark headed for Kye. Burying the knife into the shark, she clung to it as it began to thrash. White fangs flashed and sank into the base of the bull shark's dorsal fin. At the same time, the great white crashed back into the water, her mouth open and snagging the bull shark heading toward Fynn, dragging the much smaller shark beneath the waves.

Looking back at the guys, I saw they weren't even breathing as they watched the scene unfold with wide unblinking eyes. A battle cry rang out, raising every hair on my body. This was a war cry you read about in books on ancient civilizations, not the type of battle cry that's portrayed on modern television. It didn't matter how eloquent the author was in their description, or how talented the actor, it would never compare to hearing a long dead call to arms with your own ears. I'll never forget that eerie sound. It was a sound that made you want to run for your life, while also making you want to pick up a sword and follow her into battle.

Releasing the first shark, the mermaid disappeared in the churning water. The third shark had decided to join the frenzy and sliced through the water directly toward us. He didn't even manage to get within ten feet of us. The beautiful warrior surged up out of the water, impacting against its muscled body with a slap that left my ears ringing. The knife was nowhere to be seen, but it turned out she didn't need it.

Her nails were pointed claws and she sank them into the shark, anchoring herself to him. The claws should have been grotesque, but instead the long-tapered nails on her elegant hands added to her otherworldly beauty. Faint lace-like webbing appeared between her spread fingers, something I had noticed the night she had saved, kidnapped, married, and finally returned Kye.

The shark veered sharply away from us, lurching from side-to-side in an attempt to throw the mermaid off. She clung to him like a world champion bull rider, or in this case, a bull shark rider. Even in my panic, I found myself wanting to laugh at my stupid joke, but I had forgotten how to breathe the moment she had burst out of the water.

This time when she sank her fangs into the shark's dorsal fin, he jerked hard, and his fin slammed into her face with a sickening crack. She crumpled from his back and disappeared. The shark swam a few more feet before the effects of her venom set in and with a few halting movements, he too sank beneath the choppy surface of the water.

The abrupt silence that followed was unnerving. Were all the sharks gone? Or was the great white going to pop back up like a scene from *Jaws*? Was the mermaid still alive? My mind said I should be worried. We were still in the water with her, and she had proven herself to be lethal. Instead, my stone heart cracked with worry for her. I could continue trying to deny it, but I had known she was mine the instant her face popped up holding Kye's limp body. There was nothing I wouldn't have given to have swapped places with him that night.

Suddenly, her head surfaced in front of me. I stared into her eyes, studying the slitted pupils lost in the aquamarine depths. She studied me in return, her expression a curious mix of defiance and vulnerability. I opened my mouth to speak, but before I had the chance she screamed in pain and was yanked below the surface. I yelled and tried to grab her, but it was too late.

"Zosime!" Kye cried in anguish.

Another wall of water exploded to our right. The monster shark broke the surface, the final bull shark crushed in her jaws. My stomach dropped and Kye roared behind me. The dying bull shark still held the mermaid's tail clamped in its jaws. Blood poured from her tail, but that didn't stop her. She fought like a wild cat, striking out at the bull shark. I watched in amazement as she pressed her fingers into her mouth, and then sank her claws into the thick skin of the shark. The trio sank under the foamy water. My heartbeat pounded in my ears. I knew we should start swimming toward the shore. Storm needed a hospital, but I couldn't leave her.

Tears of relief burned in my eyes when I saw the mermaid's head surface. She had survived, but she was struggling. I swam toward her and pulled her against my chest. Exhaustion was etched on her face, but the feisty little vixen tried to wiggle free.

"Stop wiggling," I said. "You're injured and fighting me is only going to make it worse."

"I do not need your assistance." The words were hissed, but her tone lacked any fire.

"Woman, listen to me! Not only did you save our useless

hides, but you did it like a freaking rockstar! Human girls daydream of a prince on a white horse coming to their rescue, a fairytale I had always believed to be ridiculous. But that changed when I watched you burst out of the sea. A warrior princess riding a great white shark to our rescue."

Her eyes narrowed in suspicion when I said the word *princess*, but she stopped resisting my hold.

"I hope Kye isn't a jealous man, because I just fell head-over-heels in love with you, soldier."

CHAPTER TWELVE

ZOSIME

The giant man declared his love for me, then shushed me. He pinned me against his chest, careful not to hurt me, while also not giving me enough room to wiggle free. I wanted to be angry with him, but the truth was that I didn't know if I could make it on my own in my current condition.

The knife wound in my side had widened during the shark frenzy, and lacerations covered my body. The worst was the damage to my ankles and fluke. Skin hung from my tail, and I thought I saw the flash of white bone. Blood was leaking into the water at a rate that didn't bode well for my long-term survival.

I was in a bad position. If I were able to drink my fill of blood, my body would stitch itself back together. I shuddered, remembering the incident with boat blades that happened shortly after I had awakened. If I had healed from those injuries, then I could heal from these. The main issue was my inability to hunt due to being unable to swim, and I couldn't heal until I got blood. Groaning, I dropped my head onto Eason's chest.

"I know it hurts. Is there anything I can do to help you?" he asked gently.

"Not unless you are willing to let me sink my fangs into you and drink my fill. Also, if I drink from you, it's likely my venom will have...uncomfortable side-effects for you."

His heart stuttered. If he feared me, why would he be working so hard to keep me alive? I wished I could hear his thoughts, but my mind was silent. My body must be in worst shape than I thought for my abilities to be so weak.

"What type of effects?" His husky voice sent another shudder through me. The longer I was around these men, the stronger the pull toward them became.

"It will intensify your sexual desires," I muttered. "I will likely be lost to the Siren's nature and unable to resist my own desires."

"You desire me?" He sounded hopeful.

"Of course. You are meant to be mine, and I am meant to be claimed by you." I wanted to close my mouth and stop myself from rambling, but exhaustion had loosened my tongue. "I don't know how Kye would feel about it, and I do not want to hurt him. I understand he changed his mind, and I will honor his decision. Among my people, the bond is not something we are able to dishonor, so I cannot take another mate without his agreement."

"But if he agreed, you would want to complete the binding with me?"

"Yes, without question. I would do it, even knowing you might leave me behind." My eyes were growing heavier with each passing second.

"What will my blood do for you?" I heard Eason whisper.

"It is my best chance at survival. I cannot heal without blood. Even if I drink from you, it may not be enough. I'm not a medical doctor, but I think I am bleeding internally."

"What if you drank from Kye and me? Would that be enough for you to heal?" Worry strained his voice.

"Yes. I would be able to heal Storm's injuries as well. I can smell his blood. Too much blood." I wished he would stop talking; I was tired and wanted to sleep.

"We thought you might be able to heal him. Kye's head injury was healed when you brought him back to the boat. You really could heal Storm? Are you sure?"

"Yes."

Numbness wrapped me in its embrace, freeing me from the excruciating pain that clawed at my sanity. My heart stumbled, no longer a steady rhythm, but all I felt was relief. I could sleep now.

WARM LIQUID SPICE COATED MY THROAT, REMINDING ME of the chai tea I had tasted while traveling thousands of years ago. I sloshed the liquid around my mouth, wanting to savor it. The scent of saltwater, sweat, aromatic spices, and manly musk threatened to overwhelm my senses. Sunshine warmed my aching body, making me want to arch my back in a deep feline stretch. Cool water lapped at my waist, occasionally splashing over my shoulders. I doubted anything could have made the moment more perfect.

Then, a husky male growl vibrated through my body. Coming out of my drunken daze, I snapped open my eyes. The world around me was unfocused and I struggled to clear my vision. I retracted my fangs and tilted myself back in the arms of the man holding me. Eason's lust-filled amber eyes bore into mine. I gasped in a shocked breath, as pieces started to click into place.

I had passed out, and Eason had found a way to get me to swallow enough blood to begin the healing process in my body. At some point, my body, or more likely the Siren, had taken over and decided to take what we wanted...and that was Eason. I felt the hard length of him press against my stomach, leaving no doubt in my mind that he wanted me too.

My voice croaked as I tried to recall how to use my vocal cords.

"Did I hurt you?" I didn't even recognize my voice. Since waking, my voice was lower and huskier than it had been before the battle. This low-pitched voice was pure silky seduction. I hadn't sung the words, but they carried a lilt that suggested naughty things that made me blush. I had coped each time my body changed and adapted, but I wasn't sure I could handle having a voice that made me blush every time I spoke.

Eason moaned, and I felt his body press harder against

mine. To my utter surprise, another body pressed against my back, trapping me between two people. The moment his skin touched mine, I knew it was my Kye. He trailed kissed down my spine, while his hands gripped my hips and held me in place against his rock-hard manhood. My voice might have made me blush in embarrassment, but it appeared to have a much larger impact on these men.

Eason and Kye continued to kiss and lick at my skin, neither man seeming inclined to answer me. I would not allow things to go any further until my questions were answered.

"I need to know if I have injured anyone," I said. My skin flushed at the sound of my voice and their hard muscled bodies trembled against mine.

"You haven't hurt anyone. Eason was bitten, but he wanted that." Kye sounded as if he were speaking through a throat filled with gravel. Parts of me grew wet, and it had nothing to do with the water surrounding us.

"Kye, I need to know you are okay with this," I continued. "I can stop now but if I take more of his blood to heal myself, I will end up claiming him. It cannot be undone. Being bonded to multiple mates was common among my people, but I do not believe it is the same with the humans of today." As I spoke, my body quivered in need. I needed blood to heal, but I needed so much more.

"Yes, Zosi," Kye said with a smile. "Eason and I spoke, we're in complete agreement. If you want us, then we are yours."

I had so many things I wanted to ask them, but I had held

back the Siren as long as possible. I needed to hear one more thing though.

"Eason, do you truly want to be claimed by me?" If I thought my voice was seductive before, this time it was full of sin. It had escalated from hinting at things to come, to making you believe you were in the middle of passionate sex from your wildest dreams.

"Yes, mi amor," Eason whispered. "I felt the pull to you that day on the beach. When you surfaced with Kye in your arms, I wanted you. I'm ashamed to admit I was jealous when he returned bearing your mark. I am yours. Please."

The words were strangled but spoken with conviction. His voice had cracked with the last word, a desperate plea. His need, and likely my venom, ran wild through his veins.

Mine.

So, I sank my fangs back into his neck. My own need was a living thing inside me that was trying to claw its way out. The taste of my venom mixing with the exotic spice of his blood was too much. My skin felt too tight, and my blood too hot. Sweated coated every inch of me that bobbed above the water's surface. Every few minutes, pain from my wounds would surge through my body like a lightning bolt streaking across an angry night sky. Instead of dousing my lust, the pain, in some twisted way, added to my pleasure.

In my feverish haze, I must have injected Eason with more of my toxin than I intended to, or perhaps my Siren nature did it purposely. It wouldn't surprise me in the least. With some of my emotions beginning to break through, I was beginning to believe she hid a wicked side. Each time I sucked in a mouthful of his rich blood, Eason's hips bucked against me. His hand tangled in my hair, cradling my head in the crook of his neck, and tempting me to drain him of every last drop.

I couldn't unlatch myself from his neck, my need for nourishment too demanding. Other parts of my body clenched in a different kind of need, one that grew more frenzied as the two men continued to arch and grind against me. Their erections burned against my skin even beneath the cool waters. Eason's fingers dug harder into my hips, his breathing becoming labored as he moaned and jerked against me. The dose of venom he had received was pushing him to mate with me and seek his release. I moaned into his skin; the overwhelming sensations were almost more than I could bear. I felt the Siren's satisfaction with her work; she was enjoying his growing roughness, she wanted him to lose control.

Hands stroked along my skin, moving lower until fingers teased across the scales that hid my secret place. I arched and whimpered. Eason responded to the sound by slamming me impossibly tight against him.

"Chill, man. I'm trying to help you both." Kye's voice was harsh, but it wasn't from anger.

Eason growled. The absurdity of a human male growling should have been humorous, but my body responded to it by sending another wave of slick to my core.

"Eason!" Kye snapped. "My hand's trapped between your bodies. I don't want to be anywhere near your junk, so ease up so I can help, or at least give me enough room to pull my hand free." Kye's voice was sharp, the command permeating through Eason's lust.

Eason not only eased back, but he angled to the side, giving Kye more room to work without accidentally touching Eason's 'junk.' What a strange human word. Kye wasted no time and without hesitation, his fingers zeroed in on my most sensitive scales as if flashing lights were showing him their location.

The first soft brush had my body lurching forward, although with Kye pinning my back against his chest, I didn't move much.

"Be still, mermaid."

My body obeyed his command, relaxing back against him. It was then that I noticed something that had escaped my attention. Both men were nude. They had been smart enough to realize how quickly things would accelerate once I was given a taste of blood.

It took Kye several tries to find the hidden slit; I could have helped him but the heavy petting was far too pleasurable. With a jolt, his finger buried itself inside me. My walls quivered as his finger stroked and explored. He brushed over the tiny pearls that formed a row on the bottom wall of my slick tunnel. They weren't true pearls, but I didn't know what else to call them. My previous body hadn't possessed these sensitive spots. His finger circled them, and then flicked down the delicate strand several times in a row. My pleasure built with a speed that made me light-headed.

"Do these give you pleasure—"

Kye's words were cut off as I retracted my fangs from Eason's skin and screamed my release. The sun was low in the sky, and the briny air around us had grown cool.

"I guess that answered my question." I felt his satisfaction leak through the bond.

Ignoring him, I reached down and captured Eason's erection in my hand. I enjoyed the heavy weight of it as I worked the rigid length in my hand.

"Babe, Eason isn't feeling so well. You whammied him with a massive dose of your kinky cocktail." Kye snickered for a moment at some joke I didn't understand before continuing. "I continued feeling worse until we both orgasmed, and you claimed me. I wish this could be longer for you, but our current situation is a bit dire."

Guilt washed over me. He was right. Eason's breathing was shallow, and his heartbeat was too fast. The skin that normally reminded me of the golden sands of my homeland had turned grey. Would my venom kill him? I didn't know. Tartarus! I was still figuring out how it worked and trying to control the fickle toxin.

It was now or never. Bracing one hand on Eason's shoulder, I steadied myself so I could guide his length inside me with the other hand. His erection jerked in my hand like a living thing, making the task far more challenging than it should have been. I finally slid the first two inches inside me, gasping and sinking my nails into his shoulder. He was too far gone with the venom in his blood, and with a single hard thrust he sheathed himself inside me completely. I ground my teeth together. Ecstasy and pain blended together until I couldn't tell where one ended and the other began.

Eason's body shivered against my own, his strong arms trembled where they wrapped around me. His skin was clammy, the toxin and blood loss taking a toll on him. The good news is that I am able to control my buoyancy, as long as I'm conscious. He wouldn't sink while holding onto me. The bad news was that my fin wasn't healed enough for me to move it. I had been careful to keep it still since awakening to speed the healing process. What a pair we made—both eager to bond, yet one of us sick and the other injured.

I shouldn't have worried, though. Kye had also realized our problem. His hands shifted to my hips, and with steady movements he began to pull my hips away from Eason. Just before Eason's shaft would have sprung free, Kye pushed me forward. It should have been strange and off-putting. Instead, it stole the breath from my lungs. I was bonding with my second soulmate, and my first was helping me with a tenderness that brought tears to my eyes. I hated the circumstances that forced this situation, but deep in my heart this moment would be one that I treasured forever. The warrior who hid her loneliness behind a shield was now hidden between two men who loved her.

He began to move my hips faster, my desire galloping through me like a herd of mustangs. My heartbeat pounded in my ears, drowning the sounds of the world around me. I climaxed, stars bursting in my vision in a sparkling shower. I buried my fangs into the shoulder of the man who roared and pulsed inside me as he found his own release. I repeated the Greek words I loved so much and watched as the aquamarine light etched my mark on his chest and shoulder, a visual sign of my claim.

We heaved against each other for a minute. Relief flooded

me as his heartbeat slowed and color returned to his skin. He would be okay.

"I am sorry, Zosime," Kye said gently. "Storm is worse and there isn't a boat in sight. We are capable of swimming the miles back to shore, and pulling you and Storm with us, but we won't make it in time. You are his only hope."

He pulled me away from Eason, spinning me in the water until I pressed against him. Angling his neck, he pleaded with me, "Drink, baby. Take it all if you need to. Heal yourself and heal my brother. Please."

Unshed tears shone in his eyes, and I felt an answering tear well up in mine. I wrapped my arms around him, embracing this man with a heart too big for his chest. With gentleness, I kissed his neck and then pressed my fangs into his artery. He twitched but didn't jerk away. One of his hands moved to rub soothing circles on my back. He was trying to comfort a monster of the deep, even as her toxin pumped into his veins.

I knew in the end the toxin would amplify his pleasure, but that didn't negate the reality that combined with the blood loss; it would make him feel ill and weaken him. Tears of shame leaked from my eyes and fell onto his neck. I had to figure out how to control this curse before they grew tired of the side effects of loving me. I also needed to get a grip on my emotions before they distracted me and cost someone their life.

CHAPTER THIRTEEN

KYE

I felt her tears falling on my neck and my guilt made me sick. She must feel like we were using her, yet she was allowing it. In exchange for our blood to heal herself, we were asking that she heal us as well. Her heart had stopped beating earlier and my tattoo had burned like a fiery brand. She had died, and here we were using both her body and her abilities.

Eason had sliced open his arm, prying her mouth open until he was able to let the blood pour into her mouth. She hadn't swallowed and it began to flow from the side of her mouth and into the ocean. I had massaged her throat, working the blood down into her stomach and praying it wouldn't get into her lungs since I wasn't sure if that would drown her or not. Her heart fluttered one, two, three times before beginning to beat. Her pulse so faint it was hard to find.

Once she was swallowing on her own, we had shifted her up against Eason's chest, her head lolling against his collarbone. With a piece of floating debris, I nicked his neck and angled her mouth over the spot. We held our breaths, waiting to see if her instincts would kick in. I barely kept from whooping in relief when she began to suck, and then sank her fangs into his skin.

I moved quickly to help him out of his tattered wetsuit before removing mine as well. If she woke as a predator, we were willing to accept whatever she demanded. If she managed to regain control, we hoped to plead our case for her to save Storm. We didn't want anything in the way.

Storm had regained consciousness while we had been working with Zosime, staying conscious just long enough for us to ask if he would be willing to bond with her if it became necessary for his survival. He admitted that he was pulled toward her, but he begged us to wait if possible.

Storm was a man that walked into a room with a confidence that made lesser men cower, but he was also a hopeless romantic. He wanted to plan a romantic evening for their bonding, a special night to show her his love first. Unfortunately, that wasn't going to happen. He either bonded with her now, or not at all.

"Eason, you need to rest," I said to my brother. "The effects will take a while to wear off, but from my experience, sleep will speed the process up. We are going to have a long swim ahead of us once Storm's injuries are healed, and we may need to drag him with us until the toxin leaves his system."

Eason nodded, still dazed. He managed to slip back into his wetsuit, and then floated on the surface of the water on his back. His eyes closed almost immediately.

I could feel my blood beginning to heat, Zosi's sweet toxin exciting my every nerve ending. Blinking my eyes to clear my blurred vision, I locked gazes with Fynn.

"How is he?" I asked.

"His heart rate is steady, but it is continuing to slow," he whispered. "Blood is no longer pumping into the sea, but I'm worried that is because he has lost too much blood." He didn't bother to hide his fear. Storm wasn't going to make it.

"Drink, Zosi, drink." My voice cracked. I didn't care if she heard me beg. All five of us had to survive this. I couldn't handle losing another family. My parents, my twin, and my baby sister. I hadn't been able to save them, and I had lived with the guilt of being the only one to survive. Eason and Storm had pulled me from that dark place and had given me a family to anchor myself to. That family now included Zosi and Fynn.

"Zosime, I want you to know I didn't mean to leave you that night," I said to the beautiful mermaid. "You were so perfect, and our time together was mind-blowing, far exceeding anything I thought was humanly possible. I thought I was unconscious from the blow to my head, and that it was all an illusion my battered brain had conjured. When the guys called, I thought that was my brain telling me the dream was over and it was time to wake up, whether I wanted to or not." I took a breath, fighting to concentrate through the effects of the venom.

"When I realized it wasn't a dream, that it was all real and that I had left you behind like a cold-hearted jerk, I ran into the ocean," I continued. "The guys had to wrestle me back onto land, and I finally caved when they promised we would search for you. That's what we were doing today, looking for you. Just like I have every day since the night I left you crying in the ocean."

Her hot tears fell faster on my neck, a soft sob was muffled against my neck.

"Please, don't stop drinking," I pleaded. "Storm needs you. I need you."

Her grip around my neck tightened, and she pressed her body against the length of me. She couldn't speak around her fangs in my neck, so it seemed she was trying to show her feelings the only way she could.

"I want to make love to you, okay?" I asked gently.

She nodded against my neck, continuing to suck.

"One day we will do this slow. I will take my time kissing every inch of you. I cannot wait for that day." She only hummed in response. I felt her gag against my neck, but she doggedly began swallowing again. She was full, but she was making sure she was prepared to heal Storm.

I lined her hips up with my groin, using a finger to locate those hard-to-find scales. Finding her entrance, I slid a finger inside, wanting to ensure she was ready for me. This had to be hard and fast. I couldn't risk the venom weakening me too much, since I would likely be hauling either her or Storm back to the beach when this was over.

With my other hand I lined myself up with her hot slit

and pushed myself inside. I couldn't stop the groan that escaped at feeling her around me. As soon as I was buried to the hilt, I slid out and thrust in again. The venom in my system threatened to steal all my thoughts except the need to find release, by whatever means necessary. I fought it, not wanting to lose myself and injure her more.

I was relieved to hear her soft moans of pleasure against my neck. The sounds urged me on, each stroke faster and harder until water splashed into the air each time I rammed into her.

Mine.

She was mine.

Her fangs disappeared from my neck and her back arched. She cried out my name as pleasure washed through her. I tilted her pelvis up a bit and thrust into her one final time. The new angle allowed me to hit her sensitive string of pearls with the head of my erection. Her scales exploded into light, and she screamed my name as we found our release together. Blue-green light pulsed in time with her shudders, allowing me to not only feel the after-effects of her orgasm, but also to see it. She was perfect.

"I love you, Zosime. From now until forever."

She opened her mouth, but no words came out. Her luminous eyes stared up at me. Her lips did not move, but I heard her clearly.

"And I love you, my Kye."

She was telepathic. I starred at her in wonder. Would I ever know all the secrets inside my mysterious little soulmate?

I hated that out entire encounter had taken less than two minutes, but I had a lifetime to make it up to her.

"Kye, I need you to take me to Storm. Hurry."

No sooner had her words registered in my mind, than I heard Fynn scream my name.

"Kye! His heart stopped!"

CHAPTER FOURTEEN

FYNN

A tornado created by my swirling emotions shredded my insides and tore at my heart. I had watched as Eason and Kye fed her their blood. When the venom sent their sex drive into overtime, I had looked away. While I might not have seen the act of them bonding, I had heard everything. Her whimpers and moans of pleasure, the sloshing water that made it clear what was happening beneath the surface, and finally, her screams.

To my shame, I did sneak quick glimpses. Once, when Kye was helping the weak, battered pair claim each other, and again when Kye brought her to another orgasm. She glowed the color of the sea, her eyes bright, and her face radiant as she screamed Kye's name. His roar of pleasure mixed with hers, and ugly jealousy shot through me. I was happy for them, but I was also heartbroken.

I had never felt as happy as I had those past few days. The guys had welcomed me into their group as one of their own. There was no awkwardness. It was just assumed that whatever decision was made, I was part of it. If they wanted to investigate, it was assumed that I was going with them.

They had even been surprised by my absence when I left to pick up some of my personal stuff from my hotel. We hadn't been staying at the same one, and I had been gone less than an hour before Kye called to ask where I was. He said I should have told him, and he would have ridden with me to keep me company.

They weren't investigating me or stalking me. They were treating me exactly like they treated each other, like brothers.

What I hadn't expected was that I would feel so drawn to the mermaid that we spent days trying to track. I thought my obsessive interest was because of my curiosity as a scientist. But when she had fought the sharks, and then died in Eason's arms, I knew I had been so wrong.

I wanted her love—and I wanted her to mark me.

I tried to convince myself it was simply my brain wanting to study the effects. But just the thought of a scientist studying her or putting her in a display tank in the name of science sent white hot rage coursing through me. I didn't want her anywhere near land, it was better if she stayed as far away from those prying eyes as possible. My identity as a scientist began to crumble at the realization that science was no longer the most important thing on this planet to me.

Then the men created a plan to save Storm. As long as the beautiful mermaid agreed with the plan, it was the best option we had. I understood the logic. But as I tried to ignore the sounds around me, loneliness weighed me down as surely as if I had swallowed lead. I didn't know where I would stand with the men once they had each bonded with Zosime. There was no way my heart would be able to handle working alongside them, knowing Zosime could never be mine.

I had gone from a world-renowned marine biologist and doctor, to feeling like an imposter. If possible, I would hide Zosime from the world forever. Could any self-respecting scientist hold his head up after knowing he purposely hid one of the most important marine discovers to ever be made?

I would help them get to shore, and make sure that both Storm and Zosime were recovering. Then I would destroy all evidence pointing toward the mermaid, and release a statement saying we had found a shark with a deformed jaw. The crooked cops wanted this to disappear, so they wouldn't question me. Storm would take them all down once he recovered and finished the investigation he had started secretly.

Then I would allow myself to disappear. I would travel to my favorite place on earth, hidden from the rest of the world, and do... Well, I didn't know what I would do. But at least I had a plan.

Storm's heart tripped beneath my fingers, and then it stopped. I screamed for Kye and Zosime. I knew his outside injuries were bad, but for him to have passed this quickly, there must be significant internal damage too. I wanted to believe he could be saved, but logic screamed that it was too late.

Kye swam to my side, Zosime clinging to him. Fatigue showed on Kye's face, but he seemed to have handled the toxin better than his first time, and far better than Eason. For a moment, my curiosity flickered. Had Kye received a lesser dose because she had bitten Eason first? Or was it possible that with each exposure, the effects would lessen? I shoved the errant thoughts into the dark recesses of my mind, reminding myself that I was finished with this life.

Kye tucked Zosime against Storm's side. I'd kept his head above water, but quickly released my hold once she was against him. I had watched her with Eason and knew as long as she was with him, Storm would stay above water.

We both watched in surprise as she wrapped one arm around his neck and tucked the other beneath his arm. Water sloshed around them, and then stilled. Storm's body tilted back, his legs floating to the surface. Zosime had curled her tail around his legs, careful to not injure him further. Storm now floated on top of the water, the mermaid's body acting as a giant foam pool noodle for him. If she could stay in that position, it would make getting them back to shore far easier. But first, she would have to be able to save him.

I am not sure what I expected. Maybe I thought healing magic would shoot from her palm, or she would bite him and kick-start his body with her toxin. What I hadn't expected was for her to rip open her wrist and press it to his pale lips. That done, she sighed and sagged against him.

For several minutes, nothing happened; she seemed to fall

asleep, and a tiny trail of blood trickled from the side of his mouth. Then his lips pressed to her wrist, the movement so subtle that I thought I had imagined it. His Adam's apple bobbed with each swallow. I jumped in surprise when his hand flew to her wrist, pinning it in place. The movement had been inhumanly fast.

A growl rumbled in his chest, and I could have sworn I saw a flash of teeth as he gulped at her wrist with a hunger that worried me. Would he be able to stop before he hurt her? Surely, she would stop him before that happened, right?

Anxiety and fear churned in my stomach. She wouldn't stop him. If she had been worried about her safety, she wouldn't have leaped into the middle of a feeding frenzy to save us. Between our knowledge and survival skills, we should have at least managed to put up a bit of a fight. Instead, we had been caught so off guard, we had needed to be saved by a mermaid. A terrifying, deadly, ruler-of-the-sea type of mermaid, but a mermaid, nonetheless.

A mermaid that I longed to hold and protect from the world.

I began taking inventory of their wounds. The open wounds scattered down Storm's body had sealed themselves closed. His lips and skin grew flush, the sickly grey fading with each long pull from her wrist.

Turning my focus to Zosime, I studied her face. She was pale, but most of the cuts on her neck and face were pale pink lines. I continued my inspection, moving down her body. A jagged slash ran between her ribs, the angry puckered skin was still trying to heal. My heart slammed into my ribcage. If that was a knife, it was likely she had life-threatening organ damage. She had proved she had the ability to heal, but could she heal herself fast enough to survive internal trauma?

My eyes darted across her body. Other than pale pink lines indicating healing flesh wounds, it seemed her body had escaped injury. I began my visual inspection of her tail. We had known it was bad, but since the attack it had remained below the water. When my eyes took in the damage, I turned and emptied what little bit remained in my stomach.

It wasn't the sight that made me ill, it was the thought of the excruciating pain she had to be experiencing. The shark had nearly detached her fluke from her tail. Rows of serrated teeth had sawed into her skin and muscle, shredding it with ease and exposing bone.

I struggled to understand what I was seeing. She said if she drank blood, then she could heal herself and Storm. The blood Eason had dripped into her mouth had restarted her heart, just as the blood she spilled into Storm's mouth restarted his. His wounds had healed quickly.

Looking toward Eason and Kye, I searched every inch of visible skin, but they were flawless. In fact, a rather distinct scar that had been on Eason's temple was gone. She didn't just heal their new wounds; she healed all signs of damage.

I was getting frustrated. Inspecting her tail, I noticed it wasn't bleeding. You could bleed to death from wounds half this serious. Looking at her beautiful pale face, it hit me like a sledgehammer. She had healed herself just enough to survive and then stopped. She had drunk as much as she dared to take, not for herself, but to use on each man.

Swimming closer, I reached out to check her pulse, but yanked my hand back when Storm's eyes flashed open. Glowing eyes locked onto me, and they didn't belong to the mermaid. I held my hands up, trying to show him I meant no harm. He snarled in response. The tables had turned, and it wasn't the mermaid who was the feral one now.

"Guys?" I called out to the others. "We have a situation. I need you guys to swim toward me. Move very slow—do *not* touch Zosime or Storm." As I spoke, I never broke eye contact with Storm.

He shifted his body, no longer using Zosime as a float. Storm's upper body remained out of the water, with Zosime's chest held against him. I couldn't see her tail and worried if he was jostling it beneath the water.

"Storm, listen to me."

The narrowing of his eyes was the only response I received.

"Zosime is hurt, she isn't healing properly. We need to get her to safety and let her rest so she can heal."

He made no move to release her.

"Storm would never hurt her, and we gave her blood to heal them both." Kye tried to reassure me.

"Well, apparently you three had more severe injuries than we thought, because she used very little to heal herself. I am stunned she's even conscious; her body should be going into shock. The shark nearly ripped her fluke off."

Kye moved immediately toward her, only to be stopped short when Storm's glowing eyes locked on him.

"Mine." The single word was more of a growl than an actual word, but his meaning was crystal clear.

"Yes, she is yours," I said firmly. "She is willing to die for you, now is not the time to claim her." I hoped my words were sinking in.

"Why is he acting like this?" Eason asked. "I know we get a little crazy when she bites us, but this is insane! She didn't even bite him." Eason sounded exhausted. His injuries were healed, but his body was still dealing with the blood loss and the toxin.

"It's my blood."

At the sound of Zosime's voice, four sets of eyes snapped to her face.

"Are you okay, Zosi?" Kye was the first to speak.

"Don't worry, it will be okay," she said gently. "I wasn't thinking clearly. I've known my blood could boost healing, but I didn't stop to think about how I had ingested my own toxin while drinking from you two. When I gave Storm my blood, he got the boost from my blood, as well as the toxin that I had ingested. He's acting like my Siren, the combination must be potent."

"Your Siren?" I asked.

"What you call a mermaid," she replied. "Although mermaids seem to be gentle and happy from what I have gathered. I don't think that fits me at all."

"We can discuss all this later. Zosi, what do we do now?" Kye asked. He looked ready to pounce on Storm, but with the latter juiced up on Siren's blood, I doubted that would end well for Kye.

"Let me talk to him."

Sliding her arms around his neck, she rested her head on his shoulder. They looked like a normal couple sharing a sweet embrace. When she spoke again, her voice was pure velvet, each word brushing against our skin.

"Storm, listen to my voice," she said. "Focus on it and ignore the whispers from my blood. This isn't you. Come back to me. I want to be us to be bonded, but I want you to remember it and not have regrets. It is your choice; I will be proud to have you as my mate regardless of how you choose for that to happen."

Her breathing was rough when she finished speaking. The scientist in me was curious if speaking in the voice of her 'Siren' required energy. The man in me worried that she was taking a turn for the worse.

Storm held her against him, not a single muscle twitching. His breathing leveled out, and the color of his eyes flickered several times between the glowing green and his natural grey. We watched warily as his muscles relaxed one by one, and his hold on Zosime changed from crushing to tender. I exhaled in relief; he was back and no longer a risk to our girl. I mean, their girl.

"I believe I have a lot to apologize for later, to all of you," Storm said. He nodded in our direction, but his focus remained on Zosi.

"Zosime, if you feed from me, would you be able to heal yourself?" I asked. I was the only one that could spare some blood.

A sad smile passed across her face. "It will take several

hours, possibly even a day to finish healing myself. Your blood would provide much needed help, but it will not heal me instantly. There is no reason for you to be weakened like the rest of us. It is best we all get to safety first, then you can decide if you are willing to feed me or not."

The thought of her pain was making me physically ill, but I did understand her logic.

"Darling," Storm began, "I need you to move onto my back so we can swim to shore." Storm tried to shift her around to his back.

I knew these men had been trained to swim with large amounts of weight on their backs. Zosime's body was long with the added length from her tail, but she was lean.

"I can make my own way back," Zosime said firmly.

"Absolutely not, you will keep that fin still." Kye's tone was firm.

"I wasn't going to swim back. Sheba has been waiting."

"Who is Sh—"

Eason broke off mid-sentence when the massive fin sliced through the water between us.

CHAPTER FIFTEEN

FYNN

"Please tell me you didn't adopt a great white and name it Sheba." Eason's tone was equal parts horror and awe, the same thing we were all feeling at that moment.

Zosime tilted her head to the side, considering his words. "No, you cannot adopt a shark." Her voice was condescending, as if we were the crazy ones here.

"This from the fish girl who rode the twenty-foot-long behemoth like a knight into battle," Kye retorted. "Great whites terrify nearly all of earth's current population, yet you made one a pet and named it Sheba." Kye rolled his eyes, not angry, just bemused.

Her pale cheeks flushed, and she snorted. "She is *not* a pet; she is like me. A warrior who has seen battle and survived to fight again, a lethal predator designed to kill, a keeper of the balance, and protector of her territory. I came into her waters, and we grew to respect one another. I do not understand it myself, but we have become connected. She is near because she senses I am vulnerable, just as I would go to her aid if she required my assistance."

Eason pinched the bridge of his nose, trying to stave off the headache of her logic. "Zosi, you do understand how insane that sounds?" he asked. "Maybe she's nearby because you are vulnerable, and she's hungry. Please tell me that this isn't shark that chased you and Kye when he hit his head?"

Zosi narrowed her eyes but stayed quiet.

"It is the same shark," Eason said, answering his question himself. "Is this also the same shark that has been chomping on your victims?"

This elicited a response from her. She gasped, her eyes widening. "You knew?"

"We aren't idiots, Zosi. I also think we know why, but that talk will wait until later. How can you be so confident that this shark will take you to shore?"

Her chin lifted in defiance. "We have come to an understanding. I would not have made it to you in time yesterday if not for her assistance, I was not at my full strength. Without her help in the frenzy, we would all be dead. She has stayed in the waters near us since the attack, keeping away other predators who have been attracted by our blood."

I had dedicated my life to studying the sea and her inhabitants. It wasn't just a career; it was my passion. The behavior Zosi was describing was thrilling. There were cases of sharks recognizing divers that they form a strange type of bond with, that even seemed to enjoy being 'petted.' I had also reviewed hundreds of cases where a shark had every reason and opportunity to attack the humans in the water with them, but they showed patience.

It was amazing that a species portrayed as the bloodthirsty villain of the ocean could also show such restraint in not attacking the idiot tourists who harass and ride them, all for a photo to show their friends. I wasn't particularly fond of humanity and doubted I would have such restraint if I had been in the sharks' position. Movies and books had given sharks a bad reputation and stoked an irrational level of fear in the minds of most humans. It was important to be cautious, aware, and respectful of these powerful predators, but we didn't have to fear them.

We needed to find a balance when it came to these magnificent beasts. They weren't dolphins, and they shouldn't be expected to act like one. As humans, we have rather limited abilities in the water, putting us at a distinct disadvantage when it comes to shark encounters. But humans aren't exclusively on the sharks' menu. They aren't actively hunting humans, nor are they just waiting for us to dip a toe in the water so they can attack. Considering the tens of millions of sharks that humans slaughter each year, along with the fact that the creatures are found in all of the world's oceans, there are very few attacks on humans. There are more than three hundred shark species, but only about a dozen species are involved in those attacks.

Sharks are curious by nature and certain things make them want to investigate further. The disturbance in the water from our boat fiasco, our panicked splashing, and the blood from our injuries had ticked nearly every box. Unfortunately for us, bull sharks were one of the more dangerous species.

If Zosi truly had formed a bond with this great white, the potential for what could be learned about these enigmatic rulers of the deep made me nearly faint from excitement. Knowledge is power, and with that type of inside knowledge, we might be able to find ways to keep humans and sharks safer from each other.

"Zosi, are you sure she will take you to the shore?" I asked. "It would be dangerous for you if she took you out deeper and you became stranded."

"She cannot take me all the way to the shore," Zosi replied. "In shallow waters, her size makes it difficult for her to remain unseen. I will not risk the humans seeing her and deciding to hunt her."

"You can't be alone in the water! It will take us a while to reach shore. If a fisherman saw you—" I shuddered, unable to finish the sentence.

"I can have her leave me at the buoy, I can wait for you there. If a boat comes near me, I will sink to the ocean floor and wait for your arrival."

"I don't like it," Kye interjected. "You can't swim, you shouldn't be alone." He had voiced what we were all thinking.

"Do not forget what I am." Zosi's pupils flashed to slits and her fangs lengthened. Her features shifted from injured prey to stone cold predator.

The fine hairs on my body stood on end and my heart beat faster; the automatic human response to knowing you're in danger. She eyed each of us in turn, wanting to make sure we saw this side of her. It was a reminder that while we wanted to coddle and protect her, she wasn't human. She possessed intelligence, venom, a Siren's voice, and skills as a fighter. And those were only the things we knew about. Who knew what other secrets she possessed? The delicate mermaid we had all been fussing over posed a greater threat to life and limb than anything else currently swimming in the sea.

Her facial features shifted back to normal. The change was so swift that if I had blinked, I would have missed it. I also caught the wince of pain that flashed across her face. My heart ached. I didn't care if she accidentally ate me in my sleep one night, it was a risk I was willing to take. I loved her.

"Zosi, thank you for the reminder, but it wasn't needed," I said gently. "You are the baddest monster in the ocean, but you are ours to worry over." Her eyes were soft when she looked at me, and I realized too late what I had said. *Ours.* I didn't dare look at the guys.

"There is another option," Zosi said to us. "One of you will go with me."

"With Sheba?" Kye's voice squeaked.

I knew which one of us wasn't going back with her. I couldn't help the snicker that escaped. Kye shot me an annoyed look that only made me laugh harder.

"She is impatient. Do I go alone?" Zosi pressed.

"Fynn should go," Eason said. "My large size might annoy the shark, I mean, Sheba. Kye is the strongest swimmer in our group. Storm is still on a weird mermaid blood high. He will probably pay for it later, but right now it's an advantage. Fynn's the only one of us that grinned when you spoke about Sheba. He will be most comfortable with the experience." Eason turned to me and the guys and added, "Fynn can start treating Zosime's wounds once they are safe, and he's the only one left of our group that can feed her." His logic was sound, and no one argued.

"It is decided?" Zosi's tone was impatient. From exhaustion, not anger, if her drooping eyelids and limp body were anything to go on.

"You understand what might happen if you feed her, right?" Kye asked me. "You need to be sure." His tone was soft, not a hint of jealousy.

"Yes." My mouth turned as dry as the Sahara Desert as I spoke the one word I could manage.

Zosime's eyes met mine over the back of the large shark that surfaced between us, and she smiled.

"Come, my love."

I didn't need to be asked twice. Storm held her waist and moved her against Sheba's side. To my surprise, she didn't grab the shark's dorsal or pectoral fin. She pressed her palms against the shark and flatted her body along the length of the thick bodied great white. Her hands must have the ability to suction. I would give anything to explore her body.

"She looks like a remora attached to the shark like that!" Kye's laughter was contagious. He wasn't wrong, she was doing a dang good impression of a suckerfish.

"Come on, fish boy. Let's see you pull that off!" Kye said, slapping me playfully on the back.

I gave Kye the stink eye. I had to hold Sheba's pectoral fin since I lacked Zosi's unique adaptations.

"Flatten yourself against her body," Zosi instructed. "You are not hurting her, but your clumsy body will create drag when she moves. She does not need your help to swim. Stay tight against her. She will surface every two minutes for you to breathe. Do not waste time, take a breath quickly."

I didn't get a chance to respond. With a hard thrust of her tail, we were underwater.

I LAID ZOSIME ON A SMALL COT IN THE MEDICAL WING OF the local marine conservation center. My arms shook from fatigue. After Sheba brought us as close to the shore as Zosime allowed, I had swum to shore, bringing Zosi with me. I was a strong swimmer and enjoyed working out, but my body was strained. The events of the day, combined with dehydration and hunger, were getting to me.

I had hidden Zosi in a tiny, abandoned boat. Splashing onto shore, I rushed into the small dock office. When things started to not add up, I had asked a trusted friend to bring his boat and discretely hang out offshore. I called him and asked him to go pick up the guys, hoping that my vague directions were enough for him to find them.

I then called in a favor at the marine conservation center. They were happy to lend me their lab and medical supplies for my 'research.' In exchange, I would have to give a lecture at a charity dinner the following year.

With that done, I jogged to the hotel where my car was parked. Reaching under the fender, I located the tiny magnetic box where I kept a spare key. I tended to forget things when I was engrossed in research, and having extra keys became a necessity. It had been a challenge to get Zosi loaded into the car. She had to be in extreme pain in the small confines of the interior, but she never said a word.

Now that it was time to begin tending to her wounds, I was frozen; with fear that I wouldn't be able to figure out her unique medical needs, worry that I would hurt her further, and disgust at the part of me that was excited at the opportunity to examine her unique physiology.

"I don't mind." A smile played around her lips.

It was the first time she had spoken since we left the others, and I was confused by the randomness.

"What don't you mind?" I asked.

"That you want to inspect me like one of your specimens." She gave a small chuckle and then winced.

"You can read my thoughts? Can you read everyone's thoughts?"

"I do not read thoughts," she replied. "I *hear* thoughts. Yes, I can hear everyone's thoughts, although some people are easier to hear and understand."

That might explain the mystery of how she picked her victims, I thought. *If she heard their thoughts, she would know what sick things they had been up to.* But we had time to discuss things later.

I moved to her tail first, it was the worst of her external injuries. The skin and most of the muscles were still ripped open. The tissue around her bones had woven itself back together so that the bones were no longer visible.

"If I stitch this back together, it may heal faster," I said gently.

"Do it," she replied.

I gathered the supplies I needed, thankful the small center was well stocked. Pushing a small stool to the foot of the cot, I got to work. She twitched when I injected the local anesthetic. I didn't want to risk putting her to sleep or giving her a large dose of painkillers while she was so weak. She was tough, but her breathing had grown ragged and her pulse faint. Once she drank blood, I would give her enough to let her slip into a painless sleep so she could heal.

After an hour of tedious work, I pushed away from the cot and stretched my aching back. Her eyes tracked my movements, but her body remained motionless.

"You did well, princess."

They only response I got was her eyes becoming slits. It was going to take me a while to understand her behavior. I was looking forward to it.

Then I moved to her head, slipping my hands into her hair. Careful to not hurt her, I massaged her scalp searching for bumps or swelling. I didn't find anything other than dried bits of what appeared to be shark skin.

My hand brushed across the scales on her face. She studied my face while I studied hers. I leaned down and inspected them closer. The scales lay tight against her skin, similar to fish scales. Her scales were much thicker though; they must provide protection against some injuries, just not a full-blown shark attack. Soft light began to emanate from the edges of each individual scale. Did she control the glow, or were they a natural response?

"Both," she said. "Our eyes blink without our conscious thought, but we can also choose to blink or not blink."

She was listening to my thoughts again. It should have felt invasive, but instead it felt intimate. Moving down, I teased the skin of her neck and shoulders, trying to find any shifting bones or swelling. My relief was growing. She would be okay.

My hands froze and a flush went up my neck. I was struggling to keep my examination impersonal, and I was quickly losing the battle. Taking her arm in my hand, I decided to check it for injuries instead of continuing down her torso. Sliding my hand down her lightly muscled arm, my stomach lurched as the bone in her forearm shifted under slight pressure from my fingers.

"Why didn't you tell us your arm was broken?" I asked.

"It served no purpose. Our situation would not have improved had you known, and the knowledge likely would have caused additional stress to the four of you."

As a scientist, I loved and understood her logic. However, as a man who loved her, I was horrified.

"Did you conceal other injuries?" I demanded, trying not to sound too forceful.

Her silence was answer enough. Anger began to simmer inside me. It was irrational, and I knew it, but I couldn't help it. I hated knowing she was in pain, and I hated that she felt the need to protect us.

My eyes burned and I blinked hard, working to focus back on the exam. I held her slender hand between my own. A flexible piece of webbing draped between each pale finger. The webbing was translucent but had a delicate green lace design etched into it. It was beautiful and functional.

"It is new," she explained. "My body continues to adapt."

"You haven't always been a Siren? And this form can change your features?" I was a man of science and facts, and she was throwing it all out the window.

She didn't answer right away. I braced her arm to keep it from shifting as it finished healing. After finished with her arms, I began to examine her torso and rib cage. The exam went smoothly until my fingers found the jagged wound between her ribs. Again, I wondered if it was a knife, and if there was internal damage.

"It was a knife. There was internal damage, but I stopped the bleeding." Her tone was so matter-of-fact.

"What organs were injured?" I asked the question but wasn't sure I wanted the answer.

She shrugged. "My lung and liver were perforated."

I gathered her into my arms, holding her against me, careful to not jostle her fluke. Her hand patted me awkwardly; trying to comfort people wasn't something she did often. She was a lethal predator, designed to kill with cold efficiency, yet she was trying to ease my devastation over how close we had come to losing her, and the pain she endured coming to our aid.

"Who stabbed you, Zosi?"

"A fisherman. I had him beneath the water. Kye's emotions distracted me, and the man stabbed me."

My mouth dropped open. I didn't even know where to begin. I had seen her soft side, and I had tried to push the memory of the victims I had examined to the dark recesses of my mind. Her victims. If I asked her why he was in the ocean, would she tell me the truth? Did I want to hear her say what I already knew in my heart?

"I do not lie," she said. "I was killing him when I became distracted. The stabbing was a futile effort on his part to escape me. He did not escape. I know my purpose, and I will do what I must to fulfill it. Will you be able to accept me for what I am?"

I couldn't even begin to decide how to respond to this. Could I? If her existence was found out, would I be willing to go on the run with her? It would mean throwing away the career I had worked so hard for.

Tilting her chin back, I leaned down and kissed her closed lips.

Yes.

CHAPTER SIXTEEN

ZOSIME

"**Y**es."

His answer resounded in my mind. It was filled with confidence and absolute certainty. He was mine. I moved to return his kiss, but he pulled away.

"You have no idea how much I want to experience your bite," he said, "but I want to make love to you the first time without the venom in my system. You need blood, and I think I have figured out a solution."

He moved to the cabinet, grabbing several items before returning to sit on the edge of the cot.

"My blood will flow through this tube," he explained, holding up a long, thin tube, "and you can drink me like juice pack."

I didn't know what a 'juice pack' was. The only human

beverage I would like to drink was bubbly soda. But my mouth watered when a drop of blood appeared on his skin next to the needle. He had inserted the needle directly into his vein, I would have to be careful to not take too much. It was easier to monitor how much I had taken when my fangs were embedded in a pulsing vein.

He placed the tip of the tube between my dry lips. "Bite down gently, love. You don't want it to slip free."

I bit down on the tube, scrunching my nose at the odd taste of it. My gums ached with the desire to sink into his neck, but I fought off the urge. This seemed important to my mate. He secured the needle with tape, did something to the tube, and blood speed through the clear tube.

When the warm crimson liquid poured into my mouth, I moaned in pleasure. My eyes closed of their own accord, wanting to savor the taste of his blood. It tasted like the sweet spice of cinnamon, a treat I had tasted when traveling with my battalion long ago. The Siren was just below my skin, eager to pounce on Fynn the moment my control slipped.

Hot lips pressed against my stomach and my back arched in response.

"Be still, Zosime. You need to heal. Let me explore your beautiful body while you drink what you need."

There was something seductive about hearing him speak directly to me in my mind. I had considered hearing the deluge of voices in my mind as a curse, but I might have to change my opinion.

Fynn trailed tender kisses up my stomach. My breath

caught when he kissed between my breasts. His hand teased up my uninjured side, and I squirmed into his touch.

"Behave, or I will stop until you have healed."

I stilled, not wanting him to stop. My stomach clenched in desire at his command. Fynn had seemed like a gentle, shy man. This confident, self-assured man was an exciting surprise.

His hand teased along my torso again, this time brushing against my breast. I moaned around the tube in my mouth. Hot lips joined his talented fingers, tracing the lines of my scaled breastplate. I focused on staying relaxed, a hard task since I wanted to jump up and sink my fangs into him.

Agile fingers made their way to my tail, paying attention to each scale. I wanted to beg him to move lower and couldn't seem to stop my hips from shifting a fraction toward his fingers.

Immediately, his hand stopped. I growled in frustration.

"You may rule the sea, but when we are intimate on land, I am the boss. Do you understand, princess?"

My body became impossibly wet. Something must have happened to me while I was suspended in time. I had never allowed a man to command me. This man gives an order, and my body becomes even more aroused. I wanted to obey him. The Siren wanted to disobey him to see if he would punish us. There was something wrong with this body. Lost in my thoughts, I forgot to answer him.

"I asked you a question, Zosime. I expect an answer."
"Yes."

His eyes widened in shock at my voice in his mind. It

seemed the Siren was very intrigued by his new game and wanted to play. I had never been able to speak in a human mind until I spoke in Kye's, and I assumed that was because we had bonded. This Siren body continued to change the rules.

"Good girl."

I meant to curl my lips in derision at the ridiculous praise, instead my core throbbed. The Atlantean Queen had appointed me the commander of her entire army, and now my traitorous body was eager to obey Fynn's orders. Oh! How the mighty had fallen.

I was relieved when he began his exploration again. My body screamed for him to hurry, but I remained quiet. His body slid along the length of mine, setting every nerve ending on fire. I almost cried out when he bumped against my hidden channel.

"Kye told us about your scales, and how they hide your sex. I am going to enjoying finding it for myself."

Kill me now. My body was going to burn from the inside out. Fynn inspected each scale like the scientist he was, and then he licked and kissed it before moving to the next. My body had been stirred into a frenzy worse than any shark frenzy I had witnessed in the ocean.

"Fynn. Stop your blood flow, you have given me enough."

For a moment I thought he might scold me, but instead he paused and removed the tube from my mouth and the needle from his arm. He bandaged his arm and then looked into my eyes. His were filled with a wild hunger that I recognized.

"No biting."

I nodded.

He resumed his mission of kissing every scale on my tail. My entire body was shaking by the time his tongue licked along the edges of the most tender scales.

"Fynn!" I cried out his name.

His soft chuckle blew warm air against my sex, nearly causing me to climax.

"It seems I have found the hidden treasure."

Talented fingers rubbed and teased, working to figure out the secrets of my body. I didn't have to wait long. His strong finger slipped inside me, alternating between stroking and probing my slick walls.

"I want to taste to you so much it hurts, but we don't fully understand your toxin. Next time I am going to devour you until you scream my name."

"Please." I couldn't take anymore.

"Please, what? Tell me what you want, princess."

"Claim me, make me yours."

I heard rustling and then the sound of his pants hitting the floor. He had slid on a pair of borrowed pants after we arrived at this building. He called them scrubs. A strange name for an article of clothing that made him look edible. He hadn't bothered with a shirt, and with the pants hanging loose around his hips, I had been given an amazing view of his body. The outline of his manhood had been clearly visible as he moved around the room.

The shy scholar had transformed into a man that the artists of my homeland would have begged to sculpt. My gums throbbed with the need to mark him as mine. His hand wrapped around his erection. I watched transfixed as he slid his hand along his length. He was tempting a predator, and it was taking every ounce of my willpower to maintain control.

After his show of dominance, I was surprised when he gently moved me to the side of the small cot and eased down beside me.

"I love you, Zosime." He spoke the words out loud.

"You have my heart, now claim the rest of me, Fynn," I whispered back.

He needed no further encouragement. I felt his erection press against my scales, seeking entrance. His fingers found my entrance. I gasped as I felt the head of his erection slide inside me. Inch by slow inch, he moved deeper. When I felt our bodies press against each other, I moaned in satisfaction.

"Full. So full."

"Princess." He groaned into my hair.

With the same slow tenderness, he slid in and out. His rhythm was smooth and unhurried, as if we had all the time in the world. Part of me, the Siren, wanted to ride him like my I rode my favorite mount into battle thousands of years ago. The other part of me was basking in the love Fynn was showing me.

I knew from his thoughts that he had experienced sadness in his past and had learned to wall himself off from others to protect himself. He was giving me every part of himself and trusting that I would not rip his heart in two. We were both broken souls, but together we had a chance to be whole again.

I forced myself to relax and enjoy this time instead of turning it into crazy frantic sex. We could do that when I healed. Resting my head on his chest, I listened to the steady sound of his heartbeat.

Our breathing grew ragged, and while his pace remained unhurried, he began to thrust in a little harder. His hand on my hip kept me steady, ever mindful of my injuries. I felt the pleasure building inside me. We were both nearing our release, but still he refused to move faster. I thought I would die from the overwhelming urgency of my need, but when I toppled off the precipice into pleasure so incredible, I forgot how to breathe. Wave after wave of pleasure rocked my body, the torturously slow build up created an orgasm that I thought would go on forever. I clawed at his chest, drowning in sensation, and struggling to take a breath.

"Bite me, princess. Now."

His voice was strangled, my body had clamped around him and he was fighting to stave off his own release. I didn't need to be asked twice. I sank my fangs deep, my out-of-control hormones pumping my toxin into him. The Siren smirked. She had enjoyed his dominance, and now she was enjoying having the upper hand.

"Fynn! I'm sorry!" I didn't need to tell him why I was sorry. It was written in the strain on his face.

"Oh. This is— I can't—"

The man couldn't finish a sentence. She had broken him and felt no remorse about it. And then I felt it and knew why she was pleased with herself. When I bit Kye's manhood, the toxin going directly to the area had sent it into overdrive, muscles straining and blood pumping. She had just pumped enough toxin into Fynn to affect his erection as well.

My slick walls suddenly felt tight, too tight. His hard member swelled as his body continued to pump blood into it. My eyes burned; if this didn't stop soon, I was going to be ripped in two.

"I'm sorry, I can't control it. Breathe, baby."

Of course he couldn't control it, no more than I could control how much venom was injected into him.

"It is not your fault, Fynn. Please, don't move. I need time to adjust."

I doubted I would ever adjust to this. The men may find us dead tomorrow, still stuck together.

Several minutes passed with neither of us moving so much as a muscle. Fynn's erection seemed to have swelled as much as the venom and his body could force it to. I could feel him pulsing inside me as my channel squeezed him.

My body slowly relaxed, adjusting to his size. The pain gradually eased and with it came small ripples of pleasure. Cautiously, I moved my hips a fraction, startling myself when a moan of pure bliss bubbled out of my chest.

"If you make a sound like that again, I will come on the spot."

Ignoring him, I shifted again. This time the pleasure caused me to bite my lip hard enough that I tasted blood.

"My turn, princess."

By the time he fully unsheathed himself, we were both panting hard. He hesitated for a moment, searching my face for permission.

"Claim me." My voice had shifted to that of my Siren. He didn't have a chance.

With one hard thrust, he rammed himself deep inside me. Our cries of pleasure echoed in the stark room. I could feel every pulse of his release, my body shuddering around him with my own climax.

I repeated my chant, bonding with Fynn. His skin glowed and swirled, inking my mark like a brand on his skin.

When the aftershocks finally ceased, we lay panting, our skin covered in a sheen of sweat. He was still inside me, both of us too exhausted to move.

"I should get up and check your wounds," Fynn said. He made a move to rise.

"Or you could hold me while we both get some rest. I've never spent a night being held by a man." I cuddled into his chest and wrapped my arm around him to hold him close.

"I'm not just a man, I'm your soulmate." His body relaxed, and his arm slid around my waist and pulling me closer.

"That makes this even better."

CHAPTER SEVENTEEN

ZOSIME

T hings moved fast the following morning. It was a relief to discover that Fynn and I were no longer stuck together. Fynn checked my injuries and was stunned to find they had healed so quickly. Little did he know this was the slowest I had healed since awakening. I couldn't be too critical of my body though; it had been given a challenging task.

I had already been weakened from not drinking, I then used additional energy I didn't have to answer the call. If I had been human, the knife would have been fatal. I had stopped the bleeding as best I could, but healing wouldn't happen until I could feed myself. Battling a group of sharks was the last thing I should have done, but only death could have prevented me from fighting for my men. Incidentally, death almost did take me out.

The frenzy reopened the injuries from the knife, and I began to bleed out internally. That was right about the time the last shark attempted to rip my tail in half. I had told Fynn the truth about my injuries, but I had not told him how extensive they were.

I also did not tell the men how bad Storm had been wounded. Debris had embedded in him like shrapnel, slicing vital organs. His bowel had been sliced through, his spine injured, he had massive internal bleeding, and a small piece of metal had slowly sawed away at his aorta with each breath he took. It was a surprise that he had stayed alive for as long as he did after the explosion.

I could have healed myself in an hour or two, with only Eason's blood. But I needed all the blood they could spare to heal Storm's human body. He had come back to us, but he almost drained my body of blood in the process. Once Fynn gave me blood, I was able to start the healing process on my body again.

After reassuring himself I wasn't in pain, Fynn had gathered me into his arms and carried me to a small steel tub. It was a tight fit, not at all like the elegant bathing pools of Atlantis. He turned several knobs until warm water sprayed over me.

Kye, Eason and Storm strode into the room and froze. Kye burst into laughter, doubling over to brace himself on his knees. Storm began to chuckle as well, and even the stoic Eason tried to hide a smile. I didn't see what was so amusing.

He finally got his laughter under control long enough

speak, "You are bathing her in the sink where the lab cleans their dead specimens?" Eason spluttered. "Talk about romance being dead in the world nowadays."

I was indignant. "Is he speaking the truth?" I said to Fynn. "You are bathing the leader of the entire Atlantean military force in a tub for cleaning dead fish?" No wonder the cold tub had a strange odor.

Silence fell on the room. I glanced at the men, but they were frozen in place. My mind flashed back to the final attack on Atlantis; the strange frozen moments in time. The sudden silence after the loud shouts of battle and then the terrified wails as the sea swallowed an entire civilization. I jerked my mind back to my current reality and was relieved to realize they were still breathing and blinking rapidly. They had frozen in shock, not from a trick of magik.

"When you say Atlantean——" Storm started.

"Do you mean Atlantis?" Fynn finished.

How could these men be so highly educated on a vast number of topics, yet not know basic history?

"Yes, of course." I tilted my hand to allow the clean water to rush through it.

"Soldier, are you from Atlantis?" Eason asked. I continued washing my hair as I eyed him and the other men.

"Why are you all acting so strange?" I asked.

Their hearts had begun to race, and I was growing uncomfortable. Eason moved to the tub and lifted me up into his arms, not caring that my body soaked his dry clothing. He found a seat and sat with me on his lap.

"I think we need to tell you about the legends of Atlantis," he said gently.

And he did. He told me how my home was a bedtime story told to children, and a tale that had many pirates searching for our treasures. It had become a legend that morphed and changed—some claimed we were human, other claimed we were mermaids. Our true history had been wiped from the minds of men and from their historical records. The brave heroes, the wise rulers, the brilliant scientists, the talented artists... All had been forgotten.

We didn't exist.

I didn't exist.

Tears blurred my vision and the sound of blood rushed in my ears. I had awakened in a strange body and in a world far different from the one I remembered. It had been hard to accept that my people were gone, but I had found solace in the belief that my people would be honored in history for the sacrifices we had made.

Humans would have been destroyed had we not stepped up to protect them and fight back against the Lure. Rage burned in my chest. We had given up everything in an effort to protect the humans, and the humans had repaid us by turning my people into a silly myth.

"Soldier, listen to me!" I snapped my head up at Eason's sharp tone. "You *do* matter. It is unfair what has been done to your people. We will listen to you recount the history of Atlantis. Heck, I bet you'll get sick of all our questions!" He gave me a winning smile. "This is incredible. We will help to honor those you loved and admired. It will not right the wrongs done, but it is a start."

I threw my arms around his neck. My emotions were continuing to chip away at the cage locking them in, and I was already struggling with the ups and downs.

"I need to go home," I mumbled. "Atlantis is there. It has to be." His shirt muffled my words.

"You think you can find Atlantis?" Storm asked, his tone incredulous.

"I know I can. If I get near enough, it will call to me."

I jerked, startled by a loud thump. Peering around Eason, I saw Fynn passed out on the cool tile floor.

"What happened to him? Is he okay?" I gasped.

Kye laughed, moving to help Storm check on my unconscious mate. "He'll be fine," he reassured me. "Every marine biologist and marine archaeologist on earth is in love with the legends of Atlantis. You just told the biggest nerd of them all that Atlantis is real. He was already struggling to keep his excitement under control over you being a mermaid, this just pushed him over the edge."

They moved Fynn to the tiny cot, and then turned back to me. Kye plucked me out of Eason's lap and twirled me around.

"Zosi, we will follow you wherever you go," he said. "Whether it is a modern city, or a city of legend."

I couldn't help but smile. These men had brought such love and light into my life. Kye took a seat and settled me on his lap. Storm held out a small brush. I reached for it, but Kye snatched it and began brushing my damp tangled locks.

"After we made it to shore last night, we all went straight to bed," he began. "This morning we woke to a message from our commander. He wants us to go in person to brief him on what's been going on and to look at some data he has collected regarding our previous mission. I tried to get out of it, but the officials here have ruled the recent deaths as accidents and shark attacks. They are trying to get us out of here, to stop us from investigating them.

"We are in a bad position. If we disagree with their findings, we will be asked to show proof. Obviously, we aren't going to show them proof that you exist. It is best for your safety if we just go along with their reports. However, if we agree with their medical examiner's reports, we are going to be removed from this case and shipped off to our next mission. Whoever has been orchestrating things behind the scenes around here will get away with it."

The cot creaked as Fynn sat up. He rubbed at the back of his head and winced. Kye snickered.

"You guys go ahead and report back to your boss," Fynn mumbled slowly. "I have private use of this part of the facility for the weekend and will use the time to arrange for some things that will help us to assist Zosime in her search." His logical brain had kicked back in, ready to efficiently do whatever needed to be done.

"How did you arrange the private use of this facility?" Storm asked. "This may not be the most populated coastal city, but this center is well known for their snotty treatment of those outside of their little clique. I had a very hard time getting copies of some of their research a few years back, even though it had been funded by my boss and he was the one requesting the documents." Storm's eyes were narrowed on Fynn.

Fynn just waved his hand casually in the air and replied, "I'm giving a talk at their private charity event next year."

Eason's laughter was so loud that I squeaked in surprise and clung to Kye. "They suckered you!" he said. "I bet they're bragging to the entire marine biology and conservation community."

I looked questioningly at Fynn, but he only shrugged. Eason got himself under control enough to answer my unspoken question.

"Fynn is a renowned leader in marine biology," he said. "His lab is cutting edge, and their research provides massive breakthroughs in the field. If a new technique is announced that will reduce pollutants in the ocean, it's Fynn's lab that created it. If a new species is discovered, or new research is released about an existing marine species, ninety-five percent of the time it comes from Fynn's lab.

"What makes this so ridiculously hilarious, is how they managed to rope the most elusive man on earth into a private lecture. Fynn has given exactly three lectures in the last decade. People pay absurd amounts of money for those highly sought-after seats. I know, I could have bought a sports car for what I had to pay. Your newly claimed mate is the darling of his field. They should have allowed him use of this facility out of courtesy for all he gives to conservation, instead they extorted him. And he is so besotted with you that he agreed without question to their demands, even knowing the stress it will put him under. You caught him hook, line and sinker. It turns out our little fish is quite the talented fisherman."

My mouth hung open. I was not surprised to discover exactly how talented my scholar mate was, I already knew that. However, finding out that the shy humble man was a man of fame in his world was a shock. None of his thoughts had even hinted that he was more than a private man that thrived in research.

"Look!" Kye cried. "She just realized she married a rich man. Wait until she finds out the rest!" He cackled in glee.

I bit the inside of my cheek. Laughter welled up inside me and tried to break free, the feeling was still foreign and strange. I wondered how Kye would react when he knew the secrets of Atlantis.

"Now's not the time, Kye," Storm interjected. "We have a lifetime to discuss the details of our lives. Let's focus on creating a plan to keep her safe and help her find her home."

"Storm's right. The sooner we report to command, the sooner we can return," Eason said. He was back to his serious self, his face an emotionless mask. Then he winked at me.

Butterfly wings tickled my stomach at his gesture and my heart skipped a beat. I found myself wanting to roll my eyes. These men were making me soft, something I couldn't afford to be. Not yet.

"We are going to request a leave of absence," Storm said, turning to Kye and Eason. "If they deny it, we will hand in our resignations. We like to serve, but not at the expense of Zosi's safety. She is our priority until we get things figured out. The helicopter to fly us out will arrive within the hour. Fynn can padlock the doors to this facility, while he goes and arranges what he thinks we will need. That will keep any nosy staff from wandering in here." Storm turned to Fynn and added, "Fynn, you can contact me on my private cell if you need to use any of my resources for the arrangements. I want all our communications to be on untraceable lines only. Kye will give you a new cell before we leave."

Fynn nodded and Storm continued, "Zosi, I know you aren't going to like this,"—he turned to face me, his expression solemn—"but we need you to stay in here until we return. We hope that we can make it back tonight, but it may be morning before we return. It is too risky for Fynn to try sneak you out in broad daylight by himself. I am also selfish, but I don't want you to be separated from all of us at once. I know you can sense us in the water, but we are still new to this, and I want to be able to communicate with you while we prepare for this expedition."

I hated the thought of being forced to stay on land. I had a secret hope that one day I would walk on land again, but this body was made for the sea. While on land, I was more vulnerable, a feeling I didn't enjoy. Storm's logic made sense, so I would not argue with his plan. They were sacrificing much for me; I could spend a few hours hiding in this room to please them.

"Zosi, how long can you stay on land?" Fynn asked. "Will you be uncomfortable?" His worried eyes bore into me.

"To be truthful, I don't know," I replied. "This is the longest I have been out of the water since awakening. I am thirsty, and my skin itches a little, but I am not in pain. It will be fine. Let us get started on this plan."

"Do you have things you need to collect before we leave the area, soldier?" Eason's question caught me off guard.

"No."

"Are you sure?" Kye pressed. "We don't mind getting them before we sail out." He was being so sweet.

"I have nothing," I said and their collective sadness was so powerful that it slammed into me like a physical blow. "As long as all four of you are on the boat, then I have collected all I have, which is also everything I could have wanted."

That is how I found myself being smothered in the first group hug I had ever received. Kisses pressed against my cheeks and shoulder, hands stroked my hair, and warm bodies pressed tight around me.

I had always tried to keep people at a distance, receiving as minimal an amount of physical contact as possible. Now I found myself dreaming of going to sleep and waking up surrounded by these men. I promised myself that I would find a way to make it happen.

Then, the delicious petting from my men reminded me of something I had forgotten.

"Storm! Are you okay?" I grabbed his face between my hands. He tried to pull away, but I used the tiny, microscopic cups on my palms to suction to his face. That made him freeze.

"Zosime, what have you done?" His voice was cautious, not angry, or fearful.

"I just wanted to see if you were okay, and you tried to

pull away," I replied. "Now you can't get away from me until I am satisfied that you are okay."

I ignored the snickers of the other guys.

"We didn't finish bonding yesterday," I continued. "I thought I had to bite for my venom to work, but apparently the toxin can go through blood as well. You exhibited all the symptoms, as well as an added punch from ingesting my blood. How are you not sick? With the others, they seemed to get worse the longer we waited to—" I paused, suddenly shy and hating the feeling.

Fynn took pity on me. "We will need to conduct some tests,"—his cheeks blazed red but he continued with a straight face—"but it does seem that once you inject the venom into us, your mates, we need to fully copulate for the symptoms to reverse. I'm not sure why that is, or what part of the process is working as an anti-venom. Is it the act itself? Maybe your venom is designed to ensure the species survival. Or maybe it is a chemical reaction you release that counteracts the venom? I'm still guessing here, but Storm most likely didn't continue to experience the effects of the venom because he also had your blood in his system. You aren't affected by your venom, so maybe the answer is in your blood. None of us have taken blood from you, so until we test some of these theories, we won't have more conclusive answers."

"Heck yeah!" Kye cried. "Sign me up for all these trials! I know it will be tough, but it is a sacrifice I am willing to make." Kye's twinkling eyes caught my gaze for a split second before Eason put him in a chokehold and dragged him from the room. Storm trailed after the scuffling pair, calling to me over his shoulder.

"Zosime, I haven't forgotten that you didn't claim me yet. When we are out to sea and away from this mess, you will be mine. Rest up, my love."

I shivered in delight.

Mine.

CHAPTER EIGHTEEN

ZOSIME

I sat alone in the room. Fynn had gone to make the arrangements as promised. I told him about my last kill, the man who had stabbed me, and how his victims had been buried and forgotten. Fynn passed the information on to Eason, assuring me it would be taken care of, and that a team would arrive to see that each girl was found. I would be able to leave the area knowing the girls would receive the dignified burials they deserved.

Kye had brought me a small box he called a television, claiming that it would help me to sound more natural when I spoke. I doubted he would be able to articulate naturally if he had to share his body.

I was still struggling to balance the different aspects of my nature. The Siren was animalistic, enjoying our lethal talents, and pushing me to just take what I wanted. She saw little need in speaking unless it was to tempt someone. Less talking, more action.

The soldier in me also preferred to speak less, instead preferring to watch and listen. As a Promised, I had focused on my mission and little else mattered. When I spoke, it was concise and direct.

Just since meeting the men and hearing their thoughts, I was beginning to hear the flow in the language and sentences. That didn't mean it always came out of my mouth sounding the way I thought in my mind, but I would get the hang of it eventually. The words he called 'slang' made no sense at all to me. But Kye seemed to take pleasure in showing me his world, so I would try to have an open mind.

I had been alone in the room for several hours when I began to cough. My throat and mouth were dry, reminding me of the sensation of choking on dust during a dust storm. The water bottles Kye had pulled from the cold metal box lay empty around me. Maybe there were more, the alternative was drinking from the odd smelling tub. I shuddered.

I eased myself off the cot and onto the cold tile. Turning so that I faced away from the small box that held the water, I used my arms and fluke to push myself backwards toward my goal. Reaching it, I pulled open the door only to be disappointed when I couldn't find any more water bottles like Kye had given me.

All that remained in the box was ten tall, thin cans. I thought about the sweet soda I had enjoyed by the docks. The letters were not the same, but any drink had to be better than the water from rusty pipes, right?

It took several tries, but I finally managed to open the can. I sniffed it first, relieved when my nose didn't burn from the scent. In fact, this drink smelled amazing, like roasted fires and toasted cream. I started with a tiny sip, moaning as the cool sweet taste slid down my throat. This had to be sweet nectar from the Ancients! I finished the first in a few gulps, and quickly opened a second. I was draining the sixth can when the lock on the outside of the door jangled.

His thoughts began to batter the walls of my mind, forcing their way in. This was not Fynn. He was thinking about Fynn, but not in a pleasant way. Not sure what was going on and wanting a chance to assess the situation before this man spotted me, I looked around the room for a place to hide. The only place large enough to hide my tail was the wretched tub.

Grumbling under my breath, I scooted toward the tub and lifted myself up into the basin. I may be lean, but I had built muscle from fighting the ocean's currents every day. I arranged my fluke and contorted my upper body until I was confident he would not see me unless he walked over to stand by the tub.

The metal door opened slowly, and the man walked in. He shut the door softly behind him and next came the sound of a lock clicking into place. I didn't mind Fynn locking me inside four walls, but it was completely different knowing the man was locking Fynn out.

His thoughts continued to pour into my mind. I stiffened. He blamed my mate for his lack of success as a researcher. I stifled a snort. Well, duh. He was in here trying to steal research because he wasn't smart enough to do the work himself.

Duh? I didn't recall ever hearing the word. It must have sunk into my subconscious from the incessant chattering on the television.

I maintained my control as the man began to trash the room. Papers were ripped as he went through the files, clearly looking for something. I just couldn't figure out what. I nearly jumped out of my tail when the sound of things hitting walls and clattering to the floor echoed around me. This went on for nearly ten minutes, and then the room became still. Only the sound of his ragged breathing could be heard.

"You think you are *so* smart," he said to himself. "I know you are hiding something in here, otherwise you would have flown back to your mansion to do research. There is something in here that is valuable enough for you to padlock the door. Since I can't find it, I'll just wait for you to come back and tell me where it is."

This insane man was talking to himself. He wasn't touched by the Lure; he was just evil. Drawers were opened and slammed shut as he searched for something else.

"Ah yes. This will do. I'm sure Fynn will talk when I threaten to slice up his pretty boy face. Once he talks, I'll slice him up and toss him in the bay for the sharks."

The wall that had held back my emotions cracked under the intense pressure of my anger. It was like an aqueduct with a hole in it; I didn't have all my emotions at once, but they were coming back a lot faster than before. It was only a matter of time before they all rushed in with full force. But in that moment, the only emotion that I felt was searing rage.

It was decided. He must die.

Mentally, my Siren clapped in glee, while my warrior giggled behind her hands.

That was when I realized I had a far more serious problem than being locked in the room with an insane man holding a knife and planning a murder.

My body tingled, feeling like it was made of pure energy. Electricity sizzled through my body, and my mind felt like it could move at the speed of light. My heartbeat sped up and magik touched every cell. The humans had found a way to bottle magik from the Ancients.

This had to be what the man was looking for, an elixir that enhanced your body and made you more powerful. He couldn't be allowed to have it, a secret like this must be protected. It was time to do what I was trained to do.

I sat up, bracing my arms on the side of the tub, preparing to flip out of it.

The man spun around shouting, "Who's there?"

I answered in a shout of my own, "¡Hola! Soy Zosime."

Internally, I facepalmed myself while cursing Kye for the stupid television. Externally, I vibrated in excitement.

Confusion and fear crossed his face as he took me in. "What *are* you?" he gasped.

"That's right, you should fear me. I have drunk the nectar of the Ancients and its power courses through my veins." I propelled myself over the side of the tub and onto the floor.

"You have a tail?" His skin was turning a strange, mottled color.

"Oh." I looked at my tail and then back at him. "Yes, I am a commander of Atlantis and a Siren of the sea. Today you will take a one-way trip to Tartarus! Prepare yourself for death."

The speech was new. I tended to be more direct and to the point with my kills. Kye would be proud.

It was time to act. My vibrating body moved toward my prey, but not with the hypnotizing slither of a snake. Nor did it move with the sway of a giant cat stalking its prey. Instead, my body was so full of magik it bounced across the floor like a fat joyful seal.

For the love of the Ancients!

The man brandished the knife at me like he was trying to scare off a dog, not a terrifying creature of myth and legend who just told him she planned to kill him.

I bounced into his legs, knocking him to the ground. He grabbed for the knife as it skittered across the floor, but I knocked it across the floor with a flick of my fluke. It was harder to strangle a man on land, so eventually I bit into his neck and delivered my venom. He stopped struggling almost instantly, his body limp and eyes unseeing.

I didn't need to eat yet, but knowing we had a journey coming up, I decided it was best to drink what I could. I bit down again and sucked in a mouthful of blood. My stomach clenched and bile rose up my throat. I never enjoyed the taste of blood until I drank from my men, but I had also never had my stomach reject blood. It was necessary for my survival and blood was blood, right?

I drew in another mouthful, my eyes watering as I fought past my gag reflex and swallowed it. My breaths were coming in pants now, but I was determined to drink so I wouldn't be a burden to my mates.

My fangs were still deep in the man's neck, tears running down my face as I gagged down the blood, when I heard Fynn's voice.

"Zosi! What happened? Are you ok—" His voice trailed off. No doubt taking in the blood splattered across the floor, the ripped papers and destroyed items from the man scattered around us. His mouth opened and closed several times, but no words came out.

Retracting my fangs, I hurried to reassure him. "I can explain!"

I didn't get a chance to explain though, because the pressure of the call built inside me. The Lure was nearby, ebbing away at someone's soul.

An officer ran into the room, his gun drawn. But it wasn't pointed at me. He entered the room with it focused on Fynn.

Well, well. This was convenient. It wasn't often that the Lure came to me. And right now, the magik of the Ancients still ran through my veins.

He was about to sleep with the fishies.

CHAPTER NINETEEN

FYNN

I t would have helped if my new bride had come with an instruction manual. Maybe then I would have been more prepared for the scene I walked into upon my return. Something must have made her snap because the lab had nearly been destroyed. Shredded papers lay soaking up blood that was splattered across the floor.

Bloody drag marks smeared the floor, most of the drawers had been emptied of their contents and thrown around the room. The amount of rage it would take to do something like that was terrifying. Zosi sat on the floor; a man partially flopped over in her lap. A janitor's badge hung crooked from his blood-spattered shirt. His fingers were slightly curled, likely due to the paralytic effect of her venom.

She watched me through slitted eyes. Blood had splashed

across her face and torso. Her chest was heaving as she breathed, and her body trembled.

Yanking her fangs out of his neck, she exclaimed, "I can explain!"

I couldn't think of a single thing to say. What was I supposed to do now? We had found a way to somewhat justify her other kills, but it appeared she had simply gone into a feeding frenzy with the janitor.

Running footsteps in the hallway had me turning to the door I had left open. An officer skidded into the room. How could I explain this away? They would take Zosime. What would it take for him to forget any of this ever happened?

It turned out I didn't need to worry about him talking.

Zosime's fluke hit the floor and she propelled herself into the officer's chest. He cried out and staggered back against the wall. The crack of a gunshot was followed by the crack of her fluke hitting skin. Their bodies dropped to the tile with a thud. My ears rang as I stumbled toward them. By the time I dropped to my knees next to them, the officer's eyes stared unseeing at the ceiling.

I pulled Zosime off the dead officer and into my lap. Cradling her against my chest, I breathed in her soft beach scent and tried to figure out what our next step was. I needed to think fast. The officer was going to be missed pretty fast.

"I couldn't let them kill you," she said, her words muffled in my shirt.

I stopped rocking her. I had assumed she had snapped and killed them because she couldn't help it.

"I know what you thought," she continued. "We have so

much to learn about each other. It is natural that you would be suspicious of me."

She didn't sound hurt, but I was mad at myself. I had trusted her enough to bind myself to her, but not enough to hear her side of events before assuming things.

"The first man worked here as a janitor because he failed in his studies. He blamed you for his failures and he came to steal the research he thought you were working on now. When he could not find it, he found a knife to torture and kill you. I had stayed hidden until he got the knife. No one touches what is mine. Do not worry, he did not find the elixir. I would have stopped him if he got too close."

She had fought him to save me. He could have stabbed her. The thought of opening that door to find her dead knocked the wind out of me. I clutched her tighter, reassuring myself she was fine.

"Zosi, what do you mean by elixir?" I asked.

"I found it in the cold metal box," she replied, gesturing to the box in question. "Before he arrived, I drank several, and they enhanced my abilities and increased my energy. It is like the magik of the Ancients."

I glanced across the wrecked room to the refrigerator. Six cans of a coffee energy drinks lay scattered around it.

"That's not magic, it's coffee."

"There is a difference?"

She was adorable and I barely contained my laughter. "You are on a caffeine high, Zosi," I explained. "That's a lot of caffeine to drink at once, especially if your body isn't used to it. No wonder you thought they were magic."

We both jumped suddenly at the wail of police sirens. I looked around the room; there was no time to spare, we had to run.

I stood, holding her against me. Then I ran out into the hall and out the side door nearest the docks. The moment my feet hit the docks I started sprinting. If anyone spotted Zosime's mermaid tail, the hunt for her would be relentless. There was a small fishing boat at the end of the dock. I would find a way to pay the owner for it later, but right now it was our ticket out of here.

I jumped on board, settling her quickly. In less than a minute we were moving through the bay and out toward the open water. I felt for the phone Storm had given me, relieved that it was still in my pocket. Dialing his number, I listened to it ring. There was no answer. Cursing, I shoved it back in my pocket.

We traveled for almost two hours, never spotting a sign of anyone coming after us. My first clue that anything was amiss was the bullet embedding itself in the cushion of my chair. A second bullet hit the side of the vessel. I listened for their engines, but our boat's motor was too loud to hear anything over.

"Stay low!" I shouted. Zosi didn't respond. Panicking, I turned to see if she had been hurt, but the boat was empty. Should I stop, or keep going? I got my answer when she surged out of the water and grabbed the boat rail next to me.

"I was going to take out the shooters, but there are three boats," she explained. "These men look like experienced hunters. Their boats are dark, the lights are blacked out. They do not want anyone knowing they are out tonight. There is no way to outrun them in this boat, Fynn."

"We don't have a lot of options, Zosime!" I cried. All I could think about was what those men would do if they caught her. "Zo, you need to go," I insisted.

I clicked dial on the phone again. On the fourth ring Storm picked up. "Storm, listen!" I shouted. "Two guys tried to attack, and Zosime killed them. We made it out into the ocean, but there are too many and they are armed. I'm sending Zosime to hide—"

Another shot rang out. The new shooter must've believed we were far enough out for the sound to not matter. I dropped the phone and grabbed at my burning cheek.

Zosime caught the phone. "Storm, come to Key West. I love you all." She didn't wait for his response. Tossing the phone into the water, she lunged forward and wrapped her arms around my neck. She arched her body and flipped me out of the boat and into the sea.

I gasped in surprise as water rushed into my lungs. I began to thrash, my need for air overwhelming all other thoughts. Above us, the dark of the night burst into blinding red and gold. I needed air or I was going to die. But if the men were up there, surfacing could mean my death as well.

"Fynn, my love. Listen to my voice."

Her body moved against mine, her tail curling around my legs to calm my thrashing.

"I need you to trust me."

"Whatever you want, princess."

Her lips pressed against mine. Thinking this was likely

the last time, I kissed her with wild abandon, savoring every second. It took several seconds for my foggy brain to realize that I was tasting blood in my mouth.

"*Drink it, Fynn. Hurry.*" There was urgency in her voice. I obeyed without question.

My lungs burned, and stars sparkled against my closed eyelids. I was going to lose consciousness.

Then her lips disappeared. I barely registered the prick of her fangs in my throat. I relaxed, no longer fighting the inevitable.

"*I love you, princess.*"

"*Breathe, silly man.*"

She had lost it. I couldn't breathe underwater.

"*I said breathe. Obey me, stubborn human.*"

Her voice carried a power I hadn't heard from her before. I sucked in a shocked breath at her command... and the burning in my lungs eased. In disbelief I breathed again, pulling water deep into my lungs. With each breath, the burning in my chest eased and the fog in my brain cleared.

"*I'm breathing. Underwater.*" I couldn't believe it.

"*Yes.*"

"*But how? Did you know you could do this?*"

"*I adapt with each challenge. When Atlantis fell, I was blessed or cursed, I still don't know which. I am meant to survive. Perhaps it is so I can fulfill my oath, or maybe it is simply to amuse the Ancients. You're my mate, and now your life is intertwined with mine. I knew I was going to lose you, and I wasn't willing to accept that.*"

"*How long will this new ability last?*"

"You will need to take my blood every few hours. When Storm exhibited the traits of my Siren after ingesting my blood and toxin, I began to wonder if he might have had borrowed other abilities from me. I had planned to test my theory when we were somewhere safe, and all together. I didn't want to say anything until I was positive. Tonight, I had no choice."

I wrapped my arms around her, holding her close.

"Now what?" I was out of my depth, literally.

"We wait for your ride." Zosi laughed a silky laugh and I started to worry.

CHAPTER TWENTY

ZOSIME

I smiled watching Fynn stroke the underside of Sheba's pectoral fin. It had been a relief when she had found us the night we had to run. There would have been no way I could have swum with Fynn for long distances each day. He wasn't a small guy. We couldn't risk going on land near the bay. It was best if we waited to until we could meet up with Eason, Storm and Kye. I had been relieved to find that my blood heated his body, keeping him comfortable during the days spent in the water. We still had to avoid the depths; those temperatures would be too much for him.

Fynn had enjoyed every minute of the journey, excitedly pointing to schools of fish or colorful displays of corals along the way. More than once he had awkwardly clung to rocks and kicked uselessly as he tried to explore crevices or hidden coves. When he strayed too far, Sheba would appear from nowhere and smack him with her tail. I laughed at the odd yet beautiful bond they had formed.

Fynn's love for the ocean shown in his eyes, and he was making the most of the chance to observe creatures in their habitat. Watching my mate explore the world that had become my home was a gift. I could spend time on land, but I wasn't truly comfortable there. When I was in the ocean, the water supported the weight of my tail and fluke, easing the strain on my body. I wondered if I would ever be able to call the land my home again.

Twice while we rested in kelp beds, smaller sharks had swum near us. Sheba didn't wait to see if they were friend or foe. Passing close enough to bump us, she made it clear she was the only one hunting in that area.

The one thing Fynn hadn't enjoyed was eating raw fish, but he had treated our ocean journey just as you would treat journey into the wilderness. You did what you must to survive. The past several days had drawn us closer. I hadn't thought I would ever have this type of bond with another human. In the peaceful world below the surface, we were able to speak and learn about each other, all without the world interrupting us.

Fynn had shared news about the recent ocean mining for the natural resource the humans called 'Orpati.' I had listened without commenting, but my brain was working overtime. Was the drilling what had woken me? I was also worried that what they were mining for, was pieces from the heart of Atlantis. I hated to think of what would happen if the world got ahold of the full heart, especially while the Lure was still claiming souls. I had to find Atlantis and secure our secrets. There was so much I needed to do, but I was growing weaker with each hour.

We had been traveling for nine days. I needed my bonded, all of them. The longer we were apart, the worse I felt. My body ached and my head pounded mercilessly. We had moved into warmer waters, but I remained cold. Feeding from Fynn helped, but that relief only lasted a few hours. I was struggling to hide how sick I had become, not wanting to alarm him while he was still relying on me.

With Sheba's aid, we had made good time. One more day until we arrived in Key West. I just had to hang in there. Sheba pressed her side against me, her massive pectoral fin sliding underneath my body, supporting my weight. I continued to pump my fluke and swim beside her. Her annoyance flashed in my mind. I was lagging and she could go faster if I accepted help.

With her massive body blocking Fynn's view of me, I allowed myself to be weak. I turned and flattened myself against her to create as little drag as possible. I used my palms to suction and secure myself.

"Take care of him."

I whispered my plea to her, not sure if she understood. Closing my eyes, I drifted to into the bliss of sleep.

CHAPTER TWENTY-ONE

LOKENE

I watched her sleep like a creepy stalker, but I didn't care. Thousands of years had gone by since I had last been able to sit next to her. The warm rays of the sun heated her skin, casting a golden glow and heating her feverish skin. She was a stubborn little thing. Until this moment I hadn't realized how sick she had grown. We had very little time to turn this around.

Reaching out a hand, I brushed the dark wet strands away from her beautiful face. Zosime had always been a stunning woman, although now her features had shifted slightly. She was inhumanely perfect, which wasn't a shock considering her lineage and the magik that had been used to save her.

If Atlantis hadn't been wiped from earth, I had no doubt she would have become the subject of paintings and sculptures. Her bravery as she fought battle after battle would have catapulted her into the human legends. Beauty, bravery, and brains. It was an alluring combination. Any man lucky enough to be loved by her, was given an incomparable gift. I had that once.

Water lapped at her skin, rocking her gently like a mother rocks her child. Zosime's scales glowed, the dim light flickering, one more sign of how ill she was. Her blue-green eyes locked on mine. The irises were pale and flat, the glow that should have been there was gone.

"Where are my mates? Are they safe?"

I heard her voice in my mind. Her heart was beating erratically as her panic began to rise.

"Fynn has gone to find the others, all are safe," I tried to soothe her, "It is okay, Soyale."

Tears pooled in her eyes at that last word.

Her tongue stuck to the roof of her dry mouth as she tried to speak. I conjured a bottle of water and held it to her cracked lips. Most trickled out the side of her mouth, but she managed to swallow some of it.

"I never thought I would hear my mother tongue spoken again."

My heart shattered at the sorrowful homesickness in her voice. She was longing for a time and place long gone. Hearing the language of the Ancients brought all those memories rushing back to her.

"Soyale." I wanted to say more, but the lump in my throat threatened to choke me.

She sucked in a sharp breath at that single word.

There was no direct translation for the word, the meaning too deep a concept to sum up in a single phrase. A love so deep it was limitless, the act of offering to trade their soul for just a day of your love, an oath of love and loyalty for eternity —it was all those things and so much more.

An ancient word that was never spoken unless the speaker was certain of their feelings. The word had been used with only a handful of couples for as long as the Ancients had existed. Ancients were immortal and could not break an oath, so the word was almost considered taboo. Eternity was a long time to keep a promise.

Her emotions and memories danced across her face like a movie. Emotions, pain, disbelief, joy, and confusion showed in her expressions. I knew the moment she recognized me. The mischievous young man that beautiful summer day in Atlantis. A day that was both forever ago, and yesterday to me. It was a day I would never forget. I had not been allowed to show myself to her again, and I knew she assumed I was killed in the final battle.

"How are you sitting beside me? Atlanteans were not fully human, but we were also not immortal. Even if you survived the fall of Atlantis, you would have died millennia ago."

"I am not Atlantean."

Her eyes narrowed and then widened as she figured it out.

"Soyale, I am an Ancient. I did not enjoy the games some of the Ancients played with the beings on earth, so I kept to myself. I heard rumors of the Lure and came to investigate. I had not been in Atlantis for centuries, but I needed to see for myself what was happening. The moment I saw you in Atlantis, I forgot my mission. We spent that one beautiful day together. In my immortal life I had never been that happy or had a day so perfect. I planned to promise myself to you for eternity the next day. Before I could tell you, my father summoned me.

"I was pulled from the earthly plane and into an emergency meeting of the remaining Ancients. These were the ones who had not let their own greed corrupt them. I was told the Lure had been released on earth, and we needed to keep an eye on the crown princess of Atlantis. She would wage war against the Lure, and one day she would prevail. She was going to save the world, and then she was going to change it."

She turned green around the gills as I spoke. Well, not around the gills, she didn't have those, but her skin definitely took on a green pallor. Her lips parted as her breath came faster.

"Ancients are limited on what we can interfere with, but we watched in awe as this princess rallied entire continents around her and struck fear in the hearts of those who opposed her. Her heart was pure, and she fought with everything in her."

Salty tears streamed from her eyes, slipping into the sea. I leaned forward and kissed them away.

"I am so proud of every battle you fought. The earth has never seen a warrior like you."

My tears mixed with hers. We cried for a lost city, for lost loved ones, and for lost time.

"I have waited all these centuries for you to awaken.

Hoping and praying that the magik that was slammed into you those final moments wouldn't take away the woman I loved, or the princess the world needed. You awakened, and again you amazed me with your strength. You learned to adapt to your body, and the new instincts that tried to control you. I wanted to come to you then, but your emotions were still buried. I couldn't offer my love while yours was still buried."

"I never forgot you or the day we spent together." Her voice was weak and shook with the effort to speak.

"I have waited a long time for you to be mine. The council of Ancients opposed my intervention time and time again, but today things changed. The balanced shifted, the Lure is spreading. The Ancients are under attack from those who betrayed us. There is a war coming again, and you are needed. Claim your mates, raise your city from the depths of the sea, and declare your powers. You are the Royal Storm of Atlantis, and it is time this world is reminded of what a true queen looks like."

I had more to tell her, but she couldn't take it while she was this weak. Immortal Ancients had been slaughtered. It was an impossibility that had become possible. Bratty Ancients who didn't get their way had released the Lure as a tantrum. They believed they had control over it, and that by controlling humans they could make the rest of the Ancients miserable.

The Ancients enjoyed spending time on earth, working with the humans and teaching them. They weren't our pets; they were treated as younger siblings or children. Their joy in learning new things was exciting to us. Atlantis had been our gateway to the world, and the Atlanteans our ambassadors. We were able to give them knowledge to help all mankind. The rebel Ancients focused their efforts on destroying Atlantis, the jewel of earth, their obsession with being treated like gods turning their hearts to stone.

Today they had found a way to use the Lure to destroy more than just the earth. The Ancients' world was on fire. If we attacked the corrupted Ancients directly, we would break our oaths. A war had started, and if we didn't find the loopholes to allow us to fight it, it wouldn't just be Ancients that ceased to exist.

Humans were finding the Orpati, and that was stoking the fire of evil that was rippling around the world. The mining was wreaking havoc in the sea, even now tremors shook the earth. The ocean was agitated, and it was only a matter of time before it unleashed its rage on the earth. A perfect storm was brewing.

Gathering her in my arms, I blinked us out of existence. My skin prickled as we materialized on the earth plane again. I laid her gently on a bed stacked in silk cushions and hand stitched blankets. With a snap of my finger, four very confused men blinked into the room around us.

All five pairs of eyes slowly took in the room. Zosime's eyes glowed faintly with recognition. This was her palace bedroom. Piles of colorful cushions were spread around the room, and flickering candles cast a soft yellow light onto the smooth sculpted walls. Tapestries from dynasties long gone hung on the walls; memories of many incredible places she had traveled. A large wood shelf with intricate carvings stood in the corner; it was still full of hundreds of scrolls she had collected. Each scroll was filled with forgotten histories, hand painted maps, and stories of true heroes. I had watched her men since she had awakened. They were all intelligent men who loved to learn, those scrolls were going to blow their minds.

I had carefully constructed a bubble over this part of the palace and filled it with air for her men. The palace bedroom that had once looked out over soft green hills and sun-kissed gardens, now looked out over a dark expanse of the ocean. It was a surreal view, and I found I loved it. It reminded me of the contrasts of my Zosime. My Soyale.

I smiled as Sheba slid past the window. I had sent her to Zosime. My intention was to provide her some companionship by giving her a pet. What I hadn't counted on was the sassy and stubborn attitude the shark possessed. Controlling her had been impossible.

What I had given to the predator was an understanding of humans, and of Zosime's struggles. To my shock, Sheba had chosen to find Zosime and stay by her side, all of her own free will. Which was a relief since I had met very few creatures able to resist the will of an Ancient, and the female great white had made the list.

Kye, Eason, Fynn and Storm stared in bewilderment, not understanding what their eyes were seeing.

"Is this a 3D movie?" Kye stage whispered in Storm's direction.

"I assure you it is quite real." Everyone focused their attention on me. I couldn't deny I loved this surprise. The life of an Ancient was boring, I was ready for some fun! Joy stirred inside me, and I felt like I was that young man with the sparkling eyes and mischievous spirit Zosime had fallen in love with.

Their questions came in unison.

"Who are you?"

"Where are we?"

"My name would be challenging for humans to pronounce." Ancient names were made up of sounds that didn't even exist on the earth plane. "Just call me Lokene. And let me be the first to welcome you to Atlantis!" Bending I gave a flourishing bow. "Now, we really do need to discuss how the bond works, because you men are making a mess of it. Zosime cannot be away from her mates for more than a day or two. She will get sicker with each passing hour, and eventually her body will give out. Which is what would have happened exactly six hours, eight minutes, and twenty-three seconds from now, had intervention not taken place. Thankfully there is time to rectify the situation, so chop-chop."

My words were spoken lightly, and they probably assumed I was teasing them. But I knew more about bonding than anyone in the room, and the situation was dire. She was still hiding how close her body was to giving up. I wasn't about to let that happen, not when she had four bonded mates in the room to set things right.

They better hop up on that bed and show her some love or things were going to get real kinky. I had watched some crazy stuff from the Ancients' world. Humans were innovative, and ropes were considered fun now. That would make things much easier. I would happily string them up for her if needed. I wondered if she would like that. Maybe as a birthday present?

They continued to stare at me. Seriously, a naked woman lays on a bed and they want to look at me? Raising my eyebrows in warning, I made a shooing motion toward the bed.

Finally, they tore their eyes from me looked to where the love of my life lay curled in the middle of the massive bed. Reaching out, I felt for her emotions, needing to know she was okay with what was about to happen. She was overflowing with happiness and love. Her emotions fully returned, but her body grew sicker by the minute.

"Lokene, join us. It is time to finish what our hearts started so long ago. You are meant to be mine, and I am yours."

Her words floated into my mind. The world may be burning around us, but for this one night, my life was perfect. I was going to enjoy every second and do everything in my power to ensure everyone else did too.... And I had a lot of power. I smirked.

This was going to be too much fun.

"She has legs!" Kye cried.

I chuckled in amusement at the stunned faces around me. Zosime was sliding her hands along her legs as though this was the first time she had owned a pair.

"Indeed, she does."

AUTHOR'S NOTE

Yes, yes. I know you guys are probably ready to vote me off the island right now. Not that I could blame you—it was cruel stopping right before our fishy girl had her way with five very eager mates.... and this time with legs!

Hopefully you guys will find it in your heart to forgive me and read book two when it comes out. *Siren's Hunt* was important to set the scene for what's coming next and to establish the background for the characters and plot. *Siren's Throne* is going to be a wild ride, er, swim!

While this book is 100% fiction, our oceans and their inhabitants face real threats. There are many incredible programs out there working to replant corals, clean the ocean and beaches, protect wildlife, and so many more wonderful things! I encourage my readers to do some research and find a project they are interested in supporting. Remember, even if you can't financially help, sharing posts can still make a huge difference. If every person does just a little, imagine how big an impact we can have!

Anyway, if you are still reading (and haven't thrown your Kindle into the sea or set my book on fire), I want to thank you all for all the support you have given me! Your sweet reviews, encouraging comments, day-making private messages.... they all mean the absolute world to me! My readers are the best readers ever!

Hugs,

Sedona

xoxo

ABOUT SEDONA ASHE

Sedona Ashe is the exciting new voice in paranormal shifter romance and epic urban fantasy. Hailing from a small town in Tennessee, near the Great Smoky Mountains, Sedona enjoys reading and writing stories filled with powerful paranormal females and sexy supernatural shifter men.

Sedona is married and has a tea collection of over 300 teas from around the world, which her husband claims has become an obsession!

When Sedona isn't writing, she enjoys hiking, free diving, and photography. She shares her home with her husband and their three kids, four pups, five cats, an arctic fox, chickens, a crazy turkey, and way too many reptiles!

Nobody but Sedona says it better...

"My whole life is crazy! Scuba diving with sharks, studying foreign languages, bungee jumping, free diving, mermaiding, cliff jumping, maintaining a truffiere (truffle farm).

I do have a crazy goal of writing a million words in a year.

I dream of spending six months in Thailand and Indonesia someday."

You can find more information about the author and her books here:
   www.sedonaashe.com
   www.instagram.com/sedonaashe